# The Cats That Watched the Woods

### Karen Anne Golden

# Copyright

This book or eBook is a work of fiction. Names, characters, places and incidents are products of the author's imagination or are used fictitiously. Any resemblance to actual events, locales, persons or cats, living or dead, is entirely coincidental.

Edited by Vicki Braun

Book cover concept by Karen Anne Golden

Book cover design by Ramona Lockwood (Covers by Ramona)

ISBN-13: 978-1508859727

ISBN-10: 1508859728

# Dedication

To

My mother, Mildred Lucille Maffett

(May 19, 1932—December 26, 2014)


Mom instilled in me a love of animals

# Acknowledgements

I'm eternally grateful to my sister, Linda Golden, for her continued support and encouragement.

Thanks to my husband, Jeff, who is always the very first one to read my manuscript.

Thanks to Vicki Braun, my editor, who is so fun to work with. Vicki also edited the first four books of *The Cats That . . .* Cozy Mystery series. Also, special thanks to Ramona Lockwood, my book cover designer.

Thank you, Ramona Kekstadt, my friend and beta reader.

# Table of Contents

# Prologue

The thunderstorm pushed through a much-needed cold front, so Katherine turned on the cabin's gas log insert in the fireplace. Scout and Abra—Siamese littermates and one-time stage performers in a magician's act—trotted into the room, and flopped down on their sides. Scout washed Abra's ears, then Abra returned the favor. This peaceful interlude lasted about half a minute until Scout bit Abra's neck, and the two went flying from room-to-room in a fast chase.

Before the young heiress and her cats retired for the evening, she leaned a security bar against the bedroom door. Katherine looked out the back window, surprised at how dark it was. Even with the porch light on, she couldn't see beyond her SUV.

Once she hit the bed, she fell fast asleep with the cats snuggled against her. In the middle of the night, a loud clap of thunder startled Katherine out of a deep slumber. A flash of lightning revealed two Siamese sitting on the windowsill and looking intently at something outside the window.

"Is it the crow again?" she asked sleepily.

Scout turned and cried a mournful "waugh." It sounded like a warning.

"What's out there?" she asked uneasily. Getting out of bed, she dragged herself to the window and pulled the curtain aside. Another lightning stroke briefly illuminated the backyard. A tall, broad-shouldered, heavy-set man was standing at the edge of the woods. On his head he wore something black that covered his face. *Or did he have a face?* She wondered.

Katherine stood back, her heart beating fast. "What the hell? Who is that?" Heavy rain pelted the window glass. The wind picked up and whipped around the cabin.

Abra cried a deep, menacing growl. Scout hissed and hit the window glass with her paw. Katherine said to the cats, "Get down. Let me check again." She walked back to the window and looked out. At first her eyes focused on the rivulets of rain running down the glass. With the next flash of lightning, the man was now standing right outside. He wore a black motorcycle helmet, and the visor was up, revealing a deformed face with one eye missing. Katherine screamed and fell back. She scrambled to turn the night light off so that the man couldn't see her.

Scout and Abra—still growling and hissing—ran underneath the bed. Finding her Glock, she cautiously moved to the side of the window and peered out. The man had vanished. She panicked, *Where is he? What if he gets inside?*

# Chapter One

As she leaned against the counter in the pink mansion's kitchen, Katherine watched Jake open the refrigerator and pull out a plastic jug of *Simply Lemonade*. He poured a glass and handed it to her.

"Are these freshly squeezed lemons?" she asked with a playful tone of voice.

Jake gave an amused side glance. "Why, yes, Katz. The cats and I have been squeezing lemons all morning."

Katherine giggled, then asked, "Do you think there's something wrong with the central air? I set the thermostat really low, but it's hot as magma in here."

"Hot as magma." He smirked at the comparison. "When the outside temperature is really hot, it's hard for any air conditioner to keep up—new or old." He removed his cell phone from his back pocket and tapped the weather app. "Yep, 102 degrees."

"It seems more like 200 degrees. What's with the humidity in Indiana? You can cut it with a knife."

Lilac and Abby slowly crept in and launched to the granite countertop. They collapsed on their sides and stretched out full-length.

"Even the cats are hot," Katherine observed.

"The counter must be cooler than the rest of the house," Jake laughed. "Maybe we should hop up there."

Katherine shot a disapproving look at the cats. "Girls, get down. You're not supposed to be on the counter."

"Chirp," Abby disagreed.

In the next room something heavy fell to the floor. The startled cats shot off the counter to investigate.

"What was that?" Katherine asked, sprinting into the back office. Jake followed with a concerned look on his face. The copy stand next to Katherine's computer was lying on the floor. Legal documents regarding the new animal rescue center were scattered on the floor, with Iris spread out on top. Looking up with innocent blue eyes, she cried a sweet "yowl."

"Move over, Rover," Katherine said to the Siamese. She pushed the cat to the side and collected the documents.

Scout and Abra were stationed on the desk, standing tall and majestic on either side of the keyboard. Scout brushed her face against the monitor and eyed her humans with a cross-eyed squint.

The monitor featured a log cabin set in an idyllic green pasture with wildflowers. Jake joked, "Katz, are you planning a trip to the sticks?"

Katherine walked over to read the screen. "Vacation rental," she said out loud. "Quaint, rustic log cabin nestled in the woods, next to a pristine pond stocked with catfish." She laughed, "Try saying that with one breath. The cats would love the pond."

"Where is it?" Jake asked, picking up Iris and cradling her in his arms.

Katherine moved closer to read the fine details. "It's located somewhere in Erie County. Wow, go figure."

"Oh, yeah, in the southern part of the county, there's a lake with lots of vacation rentals. The town's called Peace Lake. When I was a kid, my parents used to own a cabin close to the lake."

"How far is it from Erie?"

"It's twenty-something miles from here, but it's not an easy drive. Some of the roads are pretty rugged."

"What do you mean by rugged? Like an off-road park, or just dirt?"

"Mostly gravel. How much does the cabin rent for?"

"Only a hundred bucks a week," Katherine said, surprised.

"That's pretty cheap by Indiana standards," Jake surmised. "There must be something wrong with it. Let's see," he said, scratching his beard stubble. He stayed over the night before and forgot his razor. "'Quaint' means it's small, probably a one-room shack. 'Rustic' means it probably has a tree growing inside through the roof. I'm bankin' 'nestled in the woods' means you'd never find it, even with a compass. 'Pond stocked with catfish . . .'"

Katherine interrupted with a twinkle in her eye, "Enough!" She gestured "stop," then with her hand still up added, "Oh, you forgot that it was built on top of an ancient Indian burial ground."

"Like that movie, *Poltergeist*. The cabin probably doesn't have electricity, so you wouldn't have to worry about spooky things coming out of the TV."

"It can't be all that bad. There's a web address. At least the owner of the place is computer-literate."

"I bet you ten bucks there's an old derelict car jacked up on blocks, and a toilet sittin' in the front yard," Jake predicted.

"I'll raise the ante to twenty bucks. We're on!"

Jake held Iris like a baby. "Why did you surf up that page, baby doll? Need a vacation?"

Katherine grew very mysterious, "Cats can't surf the web."

Jake ignored the statement. "What cat wouldn't want to stay in a cabin next to a stocked pond?" Setting Iris down, he added, "Besides, I've seen your cats do this sort of stuff before. It's a game they play."

Katherine became very serious. "What? What did you just say?"

"Which time? Nestled in the woods? Or, pond stocked with catfish?" His handsome face wore an amused expression.

"I think you and the cats are in cahoots together," Katherine laughed. "I've never seen the cats surf the web. Perhaps when you took a break from squeezing the lemons, you conjured up this page."

Jake answered vaguely, "Perhaps."

Katherine moved Lilac off the office chair and sat down. "I'll just print this page for future reference. Maybe we should take the cats there someday. I'll file it in our future vacation folder." She chuckled and printed the page.

Jake began picking up the rest of the scattered papers. Iris made a game out of it and pounced on a page, then began kicking it with her back legs.

"Miss Siam, quit it," Katherine lightly reprimanded. "I'll need that for my meeting with Scott Wilson in an hour."

"What do you think of your new attorney?" Jake asked.

"He's seems to be good at his job. He's handsome, but not as handsome as you," she teased.

Jake grabbed her around the waist and pulled her into a kiss. "You're such a flirty girl!"

*       *       *

Katherine pulled the Subaru into a parking spot in front of the Erie Bank building, where her previous estate attorney, Mark Dunn, once had his office. With Mark in Indianapolis, Katherine hired a new lawyer to represent her interests. Scott Wilson, in his early fifties, was equally as handsome as the movie actor, George Clooney. But most significantly, he was a very good attorney.

Katherine took the stairs to his third-floor office and entered the reception room. She was surprised to see Chief London and his wife, Connie, sitting on the leather sofa.

"Hey, Katz," the chief said, looking up from his magazine.

"Hello, you two," she smiled, then sat down.

The receptionist/legal assistant, Jenny, looked up from her document. "Ms. Kendall, I'll let Mr. Wilson know you're here."

"Thanks," and then to the couple, "I want to thank you again for inviting Jake and me to your home last weekend. We absolutely love your backyard." Chief London and his wife were avid gardeners, and took pride in hosting barbecues to show off their landscaping.

Connie answered, "You're quite welcome. I don't think I'll be doin' any gardening this week, though. It's just too hot."

"Jake and I want to spruce up the backyard at the mansion. We loved those plants with the gorgeous flowers. What are they called again?"

"Daylilies," Connie answered proudly. "Every few years, I divide them. I'm getting ready to do that. When I do, would you like me to bring some over?"

"Yes, that would be wonderful. And maybe give me some helpful hints. I'm not much of a green thumb."

"I'd love to. I'll give you a call."

The chief asked, "Did you explain to the cats that I'm coming over tomorrow for the board meeting? Should I bring cat treats?"

Jenny looked curiously up from her document and with a sheepish grin, looked back down again.

Katz said to her, "I have five cats."

Jenny smiled.

Scott came out of his office. "Hello, everyone. Katz, the chief and his wife are signing documents. It won't take just a moment, then I'll be able to meet with you. Is that okay?"

Katherine nodded. She wondered what documents Chief London and Connie were signing, but then pinched herself for being as nosy as everyone else in the small town. The chief and his wife went into Scott's office, and ten minutes later were finished.

Connie came out first and said to Katherine, "We just signed our wills. I can't believe we waited this long in life to have them drawn up."

"Hey, Katz, see you tomorrow," the chief said, leaving.

"Bye," Connie said, walking out the door. "Talk to you soon."

"Your turn," Scott said to Katherine, smiling.

Katherine followed him into his office. The room was a mess. A mound of paperwork was heaped on his desk; file folders were strewn on top of the credenza and on the floor. He definitely wasn't a neat freak like her former attorney, Mark Dunn, but Katherine didn't care. She appreciated the fact that he was also a board-certified financial planner.

Four months previously, Katherine inherited her great aunt's fortune. Mark Dunn was instrumental in closing the Colfax estate. There were no problems. No last-minute issues. Not even a hiccup. But Katherine needed her new attorney's advice on how to manage her millions.

Scott directed Katherine to a leather wingback chair. Katherine thought how her cats, Iris and Abby, would love this chair. Not because it was over-stuffed and comfy, but because it probably had an easily clawed-into lining that would be perfect for their stolen loot. Of her five cats, Iris and Abby were the kleptomaniacs, and hid their pilfered treasures in an old chair in the pink mansion's formal living room.

Katherine took a seat and got right down to business. "Were you able to review my email from yesterday?"

"Yes, I did. I know the board is meeting at your house tomorrow. By the way," he transgressed. "Why don't you give the board a name?"

"Sure, how about the Bootlegging Board, since the philanthropic organization will be taking care of money from my great-uncle, the bootlegger, and his once-thriving Erie business." She laughed at her own joke. "Just kidding. How about the Kendall Foundation Board?"

"Perfect," he said, shuffling through a stack of papers. He pulled one out. "The contractor for the animal rescue center said the building should be finished in early October."

Katherine clapped her hands. "Wonderful. I've hired my veterinarian, Dr. Sonny, to interview prospective vets and staff."

The new attorney smiled. "That's the good news. The bad news is that he went way over budget."

"Really?" Katherine asked, with a perplexed look on her face. "How much over budget?"

"$200,000."

Katherine gasped. "How was that possible? Why didn't the project manager contact me?"

Scott shrugged. "I don't know. I'll look into it. He said there were unforeseen problems in construction." Scott paused, then raised another issue. "I'm on board with the free spay and neuter clinic, but I think it's impractical to not charge for other services."

"But it's my charity," Katherine said with a frown.

"Katz, you have other charities, as well. I know your fortune has grown to $48 million, but with all these amazing things you plan to do, your animal rescue center will cost $9 million over twenty years. And that's just the salaries of the proposed veterinarians and staff members."

"What?" Katherine asked, surprised. She had done preliminary calculations, but this news surprised her.

Scott put his hands on his keyboard. "I've been working on this spreadsheet. It shows the cost of each charity and what it will cost to maintain long-term." He sent the document to the printer, waited a few seconds, then pulled off the sheet. He handed it to Katherine. "You might want to revise your dream list and either give less money, or cut some out altogether," he advised. "You're not the only millionaire on the block," Scott said frankly. "You need to be looking out for your best interests."

"What do you mean by I'm not the only millionaire—"

"On the block," he finished. "Katz, this county is very rich. Some of my clients are farmers; their money is tied up in land, but they are worth more than you. We have old money in Erie County, as well. The Sargent family made their fortune in gold mining. With continued smart investments, their portfolio continues to grow."

"Am I the only so-called millionaire on the block that's giving away money to charitable causes?"

"Well, actually you're not, but I'm not privy to divulge that information. Although I can see by your face, you're eager for me to do so."

"Okay, guilty," Katherine feigned a smile.

Scott sat back in his chair and toyed with his pen. "I know you've promised magnificent things for the residents of Erie, but you don't want to create a town full of moochers."

"Moochers?" she asked incredulously.

"You know. People who try to get something for free—human sponges."

"I know what it means," she said. "But if I give money to deserving charities, or to people in general, I'll do it anonymously, so how can they mooch off of me?"

"I'll give you an example. Several years ago a prominent celebrity bought a town that was suffering from an economic reversal. His intent was to help the town get back on its feet financially. Instead this is what happened:

No one in the town wanted to work. They could care less about improving the town. They just wanted to mooch off their benefactor and—"

"The suspense is killing me. What happened in the end?" Katherine interrupted.

"The celebrity went bankrupt because of his good deed."

"Okay, I get the picture," Katherine said rather abruptly, as she got up. "I'll do my homework tonight and study this spreadsheet. Although it won't be easy, I'll email you an updated list." She was unhappy, but wanted to put on a pleasant face for the attorney who had just burst her good-will bubble. She headed for the door, then turned around. "I appreciate your frankness. Thanks, and I'll talk to you later."

# Chapter Two

After the appointment, Katherine drove through Erie. The downtown district covered only four blocks. The buildings were made of brick, and housed antique stores, a bank, law and insurance offices, and the Erie Hotel. It was a far cry from Brooklyn, where Katherine had grown up. No noisy overhead subway line booming every few minutes. No city smells, hustle or bustle, or cars honking. She drove home and parked under the carport. She slowly walked to the front of the house and marveled at how beautiful it was. The mansion was built in an era where fine craftsmanship reigned.

The previous December, Katherine had been so traumatized by having to shoot Patricia Marston, she thought of moving from the pink mansion and turning it into a museum/gift shop. But with the help of a grief counselor, she was getting back on her feet and planned to live in the Queen Anne Victorian for a long time.

Climbing up the steps, Katherine headed to the porch swing to wait for the counselor to arrive. Today was their last session. After a few minutes, the counselor zipped in front of the house and parked her blue Ford Fiesta. She leapt out of the car and raced up the sidewalk. "Katz, hello! I'm having the most grandest day! How about you?"

Sally Marvel—grief counselor extraordinaire—was short and in her early forties, with a mane of long, blond curly hair. She was dressed flamboyantly in a brightly colored dress. She was always effervescent, bubbly and positive. Katherine loved her.

Last December, after the fatal shooting, Katherine had become depressed and morose. Her friend, Detective Linda Martin, recommended that Sally come to the pink mansion to provide weekly counseling sessions. Sally worked for both the police department and the local high school. Sally insisted that their sessions occur in the very room where Katherine took the life of another human being. Although Jake and the cats tried to help her work through the disturbing issues, it took a professional like Sally to truly pull her out of it.

"Hi, Sally. Yes, it's a grand day. Come in. I'll get us some iced tea. Want lemon in yours?"

"I wouldn't have it any other way."

Katherine held the door for her. "Since this is our last time together, can we sit in the parlor?"

"No, my dear, being in the room where the shooting happened, and being able to associate the space with other memories, has been the best part of your recovery. I'll see you in a second." Sally opened the pocket door to the living room and walked in. She found a seat on the famous wingback chair—one of the few original pieces of furniture that remained in the room.

A few minutes later, Katherine returned with iced tea in a blue retro aluminum pitcher; beads of condensation had already formed and ran down its side. Two matching metallic tumblers were brightly colored in blue and red.

She set the pitcher down on a glass-topped table. After pouring the drinks and handing one to Sally, Katherine said, "I'm thinking about taking a mini vacation, by myself. I've decided against going to Savannah with Jake. I haven't told him yet. You're the first to know."

Sally knew the details of the upcoming trip. Jake was a history professor at the city university, and was presenting a paper while attending a conference in Savannah. He'd asked Katherine to go with him.

Katherine sat on a white faux-leather sofa; she sank into the plush cushion. Lilac and Abby jumped up and cuddled in their cozy cat bed next to her.

Sally asked, "Is this something we should talk about?"

"Yes, I think it would be helpful." Katherine unconsciously looked at the site where Jake had been shot. Previously the oak floor was partially covered with imported oriental rugs. Now it had modern wall-to-wall, cut-pile carpeting. "I want to go, but I think that Jake and I need some time away from each other. He's pressing me to sign a prenuptial agreement his attorney drafted, and I'm dragging my feet."

"Katz, I don't really have much knowledge about such things, but isn't it pretty much standard procedure for couples who have a great deal of money to enter into a prenup?"

"If our marriage ends in divorce, Jake doesn't want a penny of my fortune."

"Have you discussed this with him?"

"Yes, but the conversation always ends with Jake's plea for me to sign it. That's one aspect. The other involves his mother, Cora. She can be very overbearing at times, and she's trying to force her ideas on me about the wedding."

"Wedding?" Sally asked. "Have you two set the date?"

"No, we haven't. So you see, I just want to get away for a few days."

"Where are you going?" Sally asked, taking a sip of her tea.

"I rented a cabin south of here. It's on a pond. I thought I'd take a few books and get back with nature. No cell, texting, or computer—just a few peaceful days to reflect on my life." Katherine smiled.

"Katz, it's good to see you smiling. Are you taking the cats?"

"Surprisingly, no."

Lilac woke up and me-yowled loudly.

"Okay, Lilac, can we keep this our secret?"

"Me-yowl," which sounded like a 'no.' Lilac got up, jumped to the floor, stretched, then left the room. Abby raised her paw over the cozy and patted Katherine on the arm.

"Abigail, you're such a sweet girl."

Sally laughed. "I think your cats understand English."

Katherine's smile widened in agreement.

Sally grew serious. "Katz, in the last few years, you've had many stressful events in your life. You've lost both of your parents. You've inherited a fortune, moved from a Manhattan apartment to a Victorian mansion in a small town. I know life hasn't been easy for you—your ex-fiancé's murder in your basement, discovering Vivian Marston's body, and the fatal shooting of Patricia. These kinds of stress clusters would take an emotional toll on anyone, but I've seen you cope with each and every one of them. When I first met you, you felt so guilty, you couldn't even laugh."

Katherine noted, "I'll always feel guilty, but I'm not going to let what happened consume my life. In your words, all of that is 'water under the bridge.'"

"So, are you comfortable being in this room?" Sally asked.

"Yes, most of the time. Jake and the cats make it okay. We have movie nights in here, just like old times, when I first started dating Jake. My cats are sensitive creatures. If the room wasn't okay, they'd let me know if the ghost of Patricia Marston haunts the place."

"That's not what I meant. Are you comfortable sitting in here without thinking about the traumatic events of that day?"

"I have to admit, it's not my favorite room."

"That's normal, Katz, but getting back to your reference to Patricia Marston's ghost haunting you. Do you think she haunts the room?"

"No, but whenever Colleen, my spirit-hunting friend, comes over, I won't let her in here."

"Why is that?"

"Because she'd bring her equipment and try to conjure up Patricia so she could communicate with her. Who wants that? Patricia Marston, who tried to kill the love of my life, is where she belongs—in hell," Katherine said a little too forcibly.

"A little bit of anger is a good sign. Are you feeling more angry since our last visit?"

Katherine finally poured herself a glass of tea and took several sips. "No, not at all."

"Is there anything else you want to talk to me about?"

"Can't think of anything."

"Well, that about wraps things up. Katz, if there ever is a time when you need to talk to me, I'm available twenty-four/seven." Sally got up and grabbed her bag. "Thank you so much for the tea, and have fun on your cabin retreat."

Katherine escorted Sally to the door. "Thank you. I appreciate everything you have done for me. Take care now." She shut the door and sighed with relief. "I am so glad that's over," she said out loud. "No more rehashing the worst thing that ever happened to me. Cats? Where's my cats? I need a group hug."

Scout and Abra joined her in the atrium. "Ma-waugh," Scout cried in agreement.

Katherine sat down on the floor and drew Scout and Abra close. She kissed them on the head. "I love you girls."

*       *       *

The newly formed Kendall Foundation Board was having its first meeting in the dining room. Katherine had deliberately shut the door to the kitchen so the cats wouldn't interrupt the meeting. Scout, Abra and Iris stood on the other side of the door and took turns jiggling the doorknob, pawing the door and throwing themselves against it.

"No, you cannot come in!" Katherine said sternly. The doorbell rang so she moved to answer it. Chief London had just arrived with Margie Cokenberger. "Come in," Katherine said, directing them to the dining room.

"Thanks for arranging a time around my work schedule," the chief began. "I'm training a new officer and it's been very hectic down at the station."

"I thought you were saving that position for me," Katherine joked. The chief had asked her several times to join the force or be a consultant.

"Hey, kiddo," Margie said.

"Hi, Margie. How are you this fine day?"

"I'm so tired. I've been working on this old house on Mercer Street. It's got a lot of oak interior doors covered with layers of paint. Each one has to be stripped and re-stained." Margie was an ace at restoring old houses.

"Everyone have a seat. We can begin." Katherine passed several documents around the table.

The chief said curiously, "So, this is it? Three people? I thought there was a fourth person."

Katherine's face reddened. "There was, but he later declined." Katherine referred to Jake's refusal to serve on the board for various reasons, none of which made any sense to her.

Margie gave a knowing look, but didn't say anything. Katherine made a mental note to ask her later.

The cats on the other side of the door began hissing and fighting. A tremendous crash came from the kitchen.

"Excuse me," Katherine said, getting up and heading to the door.

Margie said, "Katz, they're really duking it out over there."

Chief added, "Just let them in. They won't bother us."

Katherine knew from experience that there was nothing more annoying to a cat than being locked behind a closed door with its human on the other side. In Katherine's case, it was several cats conspiring to get over.

She opened the door and waded through excited felines. Her retro aluminum pitcher had been knocked off the counter, and had rolled to a stop in front of the refrigerator. While Katherine put the pitcher back on the counter, Scout led the group of five miscreants into the dining room.

The chief said, amused, "Talk about premeditation. I see the big brown one is the ringleader."

Katherine grinned. "That's Scout. You met her once during unpleasant circumstances."

The chief tugged his beard as he remembered the Vivian Marston murder case. "Yeah, I thought your cat had rabies."

Katherine shrugged off the bad memory and continued to introduce the rest of the cats. Lilac and Abby sprang to the table, stretched up to full height, then effortlessly leaped on top of the china hutch.

"Whoosh," Margie said, looking overhead. "My cat, Spitty, is too fat to do that."

"Okay, that's two out of our way," Katherine said, looking up at Lilac and Abby. Iris slinked behind Chief London's chair and looked suspiciously at his back pocket. Katherine gave her a look of, 'Don't even think about it.' Iris sassed back a loud 'yowl.'

"Waugh," Scout scolded Iris, who retreated to the dining room corner. Scout sprang up to one of the Eastlake side chairs pushed up against the wainscoting; Abra joined her.

Katherine glanced at her watch. "Let's begin with the obvious. I've inherited a fortune. I cannot fathom having all of this money. Plain and simple—I want to get rid of some of it."

The chief and Margie looked at Katherine with rapt attention.

The chief joked, "I can think about what I'd do with millions of dollars. I'd blow this Popsicle stand in a second. Buy me a beach-front home in Malibu. Sit around in luxury with my wife, drinkin' a Mai Tai."

"That sounds like a great dream," Katherine said, pulling an envelope out of a manila folder. She slid the envelope over to the chief.

"What's this?" he asked curiously.

"Open it," Katherine said.

"Okay," he said, slitting the seal. He extracted a computer printout of a vacation resort hotel in Hawaii, along with two prepaid airline tickets. His jaw dropped open, "What the heck?"

"Little birdie told me you and the wife needed a little vacation. Two weeks. You pick the dates."

"Oh, Katz, I can't accept this," the chief pleaded.

"It's not from me. Read the address on the back of the envelope."

"The Kendall cats." The chief emitted a laugh, punctuated with short snorts. "Thank you."

Scout answered, "Ma-waugh."

Everyone at the table laughed.

Katherine looked at Margie. "Two little birdies told me you'd be needing a vacation, too."

Margie's eyes grew big. "Katz, what have you up and done?"

"The Kendall cats consulted with Tommy and Shelly. Your kids voted for a trip down south." Katherine slid an envelope to Margie.

Margie slowly opened it. It was a rare treat when Cokey and she could find the time to go on vacation, but with the kids out of school, it would be the perfect time. "Bless your heart! Disney World. We'll be stayin' right there at the theme park. Oh, my goodness. Itineraries, boarding passes, and tickets to the parks," she said excitedly. She jumped out of her seat and rushed over and hugged Katherine. "I love you, kiddo. Thanks so much." Returning to her seat, she said to the felines, "Oh, I love you, too. Thank you, cats."

Katherine said happily, "Both of you are quite welcome, so now let's begin the meeting. Because I don't know many people in the town, I'd like the two of you to be my Erie pulse. I want to know where my money will do the most good in helping people who find themselves in distress. Who gets it, and how? I've lived in Erie long enough to know that people don't always take kindly to charity, so we have to discover ways of finding those who truly deserve help, and weed out potential moochers."

The chief chuckled. "Moochers. I like that word."

"Katz, I have a few ideas of my own," Margie said. "There's some really poor people who live in Erie. Most of them can't afford to heat their homes in the winter, so they resort to burning logs in their fireplaces—that is, if they are lucky to have a fireplace—or use kerosene heaters. I don't know if you are aware about the dangers of kerosene, but it's one of the most explosive fuels on this planet."

The chief interjected, "I think Margie is referring to the houses down by the tracks. The Smiths have six children, ranging in ages from two to twelve. I know about them because the kid's father, Kyle, has been in and out of trouble with the law for years. Right now he's under house arrest for being a habitual DUI driver. He stays at home with the kids while his wife, Debbie, works at the diner."

Katherine said, "I don't know a Debbie at the diner."

"That's because she works in the kitchen. She's the cook's helper—assistant, or whatever."

"How can my fortune help—?"

Margie finished the sentence, "—without it seeming like charity."

The chief said, "Debbie needs a car—one that will accommodate her family. Last winter, I'd see her walking to the diner in a foot of snow. That's a good mile. I'd pick her up sometimes and take her to wherever she needed to go; so did my officers, but we can't be there for her all the time."

Katherine smiled. "Poor soul. She must be exhausted before she even makes it to the workplace. Chief, I like your idea. I'll buy her a minivan and have it delivered. I want to do this as an anonymous donation."

"Anonymous because of the moocher factor," the Chief laughed.

"When you get a chance, I need a list of the needy from you two. Personally, I'll have great fun with this, so I need a name a month."

Margie offered, "Many of the needy are not computer savvy to apply for government help. My friend Susan's mother has dementia, and needs to be placed in a nursing home. She doesn't have any money, so Susan was at a loss about how to go about it. There are agency offices, but you have to have a lot of documentation to prove who you are. Much of this information is on the Internet. Susan doesn't know how to use the computer."

Katherine thought for a moment. "Because I'm still doing my computer training course, maybe I can come up with an idea of paid processors to help the elderly and their children find the help they need."

Margie smiled. "I think that's a fantastic idea."

Katherine smiled. "And, my crowning achievement—drum roll, please—the animal rescue center should be finished in early October."

"Bravo!" Margie complimented.

"I second that," the chief said. "I have several questions. Is the center for just the critters in Erie, or for the entire county?"

"County," Katherine explained. "I foresee working with neighboring counties, as well."

"Is it just for cats and dogs?"

"No, I plan on other animals, as well—whatever creature is in need. It could be an elephant or a snow leopard."

"Not likely in Erie," Margie laughed.

"Actually, there will be areas for horses, cattle, sheep—I mean larger animals."

"Erie's Ark," the chief tipped his head back and snorted.

Scout and Abra looked at him with great interest, then at the floor, where Iris was deftly pawing the chief's back pocket, attempting to extract a protruding set of keys.

Katherine saw the gesture and looked under the table at the Siamese thief. "Iris," she scolded.

The chief turned in his chair and observed the pickpocket. "I heard about you," he said to Iris. He grabbed his keys while Iris scampered off. "You're the one I need to make the handcuffs for," he called after the mischievous cat.

Katherine corrected, "That was Abby. However, they are both thieves. Better check your pockets to make sure she didn't steal anything else."

The chief patted his back pockets, "Nope, everything is where it's supposed to be," then the chief coughed nervously. "Not to bring you down, Katz, but there's been some gossip around town about the new rescue center. I call it mean-spirited diner talk. You might want to watch your back."

"What do you mean?" Katherine asked, shocked.

"The folks down at the Erie animal shelter are spitting bullets, if you catch my drift. In particular, Melanie, who manages it, is afraid she'll be out of a job."

42

"Yes, I know," Katherine said. "I ran into her on the street yesterday. She was very angry until I told her the entire staff would find jobs at the new center."

Margie countered, "Are you sure, Katz, you want to hire these people?"

"Why?"

"Well, because they're wonderful with animals, but terrible with people. Melanie is the biggest snot in Erie."

"I fully understand where you're coming from. When Iris went missing, I was at the shelter several times a day. I know from firsthand experience I was a pain in their side. But their hostility had nothing to do with me—at least I want to believe that—but because they are so overwhelmed. They have such limited staff to deal with the kind of problems they shouldn't have to shoulder. It's a zoo down there. Did you know the intake area for cats and dogs is in the *same* room? The poor cats were freaked out by the barking."

"I hear ya," the chief agreed. "Here's my two cents worth. Send the Erie shelter staff to some kind of customer awareness training in the city."

"You read my mind," Katherine agreed.

The chief wasn't quite finished. "What's the town of Erie supposed to do with the old shelter?"

Margie said, cynically. "Burn the damn thing down to the ground."

"Maybe the fire department could practice on the building?" Katherine suggested.

The chief chuckled. "We'll let the Mayor figure it out."

Katherine said, "Okay, I think that just about winds things up. Thank you for coming. I'll email you when we'll have the next meeting."

"Thank ya, ma'am," the chief said. "I'll let myself out. I think you have something to ask Margie," he winked and left.

"Well, Katz, I got something to tell ya, and it ain't good. People down at the diner are not only badmouthing you, but also my nephew. They're sayin' that Jake's just after your money. I know it's ridiculous, but . . ."

Katherine gave a dejected look. "Between you and me, I think that's why Jake's pushing the prenup on me. I don't want to sign it. That's why we haven't set the date. I love Jake so much. I don't want a piece of paper to come between us."

"I know, Katz, but I also know that Jake loves you. And he'll do anything to keep idiot people in this town from saying bad things about you."

"Maybe our next meeting should be at the diner to get the Erie pulse," Katherine joked, trying to return the mood back to happy.

Margie didn't laugh, but added seriously, "It's probably none of my business, but why are you being so charitable in Erie? It's not like folks have been very kind to you. Why not donate back east where you come from?"

"I'm in the process of setting that up. Since I'm from Bay Ridge, Brooklyn, I want to sponsor an annual academic scholarship fund for the technical college there. The cost of putting a student through college or university is a lot more expensive than it is in this state. But, back to Erie, I want to give back to the town what my great uncle stole from them."

"That bootlegging business was eons ago," Margie said.

"I know, but not forgotten. Well, at least not by me."

"Okay, kiddo. I've got to get goin'. Those old doors aren't gonna stain themselves."

Katherine walked Margie to the door with Iris following close behind. Margie left and Katherine picked up the Siamese, "Are you sad you didn't find anything to steal from the chief?" she joked.

"Yowl," Iris sassed.

"No, Miss Siam, I don't think the chief's Glock would have been such a good idea."

# Chapter Three

Katherine sat on the front porch swing at the pink mansion. She was sipping a glass of chilled Moscato, waiting for Jake to pick her up. Jake's parents, Johnny and Cora, had invited them to dinner. Jake was teaching a late-afternoon history class and was running late.

Her cell phone rang, so she stopped swinging to answer. She read the name on the screen. "Hello, Colleen. How's the Big Apple without me?" Colleen and Daryl had driven to Manhattan so Colleen could show him the town.

Colleen answered with a question. "Katz, guess what Daryl and I are doing?"

"Taking a guided tour of the Statue of Liberty?" she quipped.

"We're sitting in a booth at O'Flannery Pub, eating Irish soda bread and waiting for our fish and chips."

"I'm so jealous," Katherine answered. "Are you two having a good time?"

"Yes, but I think Daryl is suffering culture shock. He keeps looking up at the buildings in awe. I'm afraid he'll wrench his neck."

"How long are you two staying?"

"We're driving back in a week. Daryl wants to stay overnight in Ohio somewhere to go to a car show. Supposedly, it's the event of the season," Colleen snickered.

"Is Daryl going to show his Impala?" Daryl drove a restored 1967 four-door white Impala.

"No, it's also a swap meet. Daryl's looking for some part for his car. Oh, before I forget, guess what Mum did?"

Katherine thought, *Hard telling.*

Colleen countered, "I heard that."

Katherine and Colleen had been friends since elementary school and often picked up on each other's thoughts.

"Katz, Mum is doing grand. The counseling really helped and she's attending the local AA meetings."

"Okay, sorry."

"She flew to Ireland to visit Aunt Eileen. Jacky went with her. So, Daryl and I have the apartment to ourselves."

"Great," Katherine said noncommittally.

"Okay, what gives?" Colleen asked, suspecting Katz was hiding something from her.

"Is it that obvious?"

"Has it got something to do with the Cora-monster?"

"Sort of," Katherine said, disappointed.

"What has she done now?"

"She wants to run the wedding show. I just want a quiet wedding at the mansion, but she wants something rivaling Disney World. I can see Mickey Mouse and an entourage of mice, descending the steps of the pink mansion, singing the Mouseketeers song."

"With the cats in hot pursuit," Colleen laughed. "I wouldn't worry about it, Katz. You two haven't set the date. So stall her. What else are you not telling me?"

"Jake has a seminar to attend in Savannah; he's presenting a paper. I was supposed to go, but I've changed my mind. I haven't told him yet."

"For the love of Mary, you'd rather stay at home and miss out on a trip out of Erie with the man in your life?"

"I'm not staying at home. I rented a cabin out in the country."

"Shut the door!" Colleen said incredulously. "A cabin? Seriously? Are you taking a bodyguard?"

"Miss Glock will do me just fine."

"I hope the cabin has room for you and the cats."

"I'm not taking them. It's just me. My grief counselor agreed that it would be good for me to have some alone time."

"I understand. Listen, Katz, our food just arrived and Daryl is giving me a 'I'm starved' look. Talk to you later." Colleen hung up.

Jake pulled up in his Jeep Wrangler. Katherine bounded down the steps and climbed into the Jeep. She leaned over and kissed him on the cheek.

Jake said, "I love it when you do that. It makes me feel like a real chauffeur."

She burst out laughing. "Like the one who used to drive my great aunt around. Too funny!"

"Yeah," he said, then became serious. "Katz, beware. My mom is on high alert. Too much caffeine, too much chocolate, but she's full of it."

"I'll consider myself warned."

When Jake and Katherine parked in front of his parents' American four-square, his father Johnny met them. He opened Katherine's door and she got out. "Hello, Ms. Katz," he said. "Follow me." Jake joined the two of them on the sidewalk.

After they discussed the horrid heat, Johnny escorted the couple to an all-season sun porch. A table set for four was handsomely appointed with a crisp white tablecloth, and a table setting rivaling any home and garden magazine. It was apparent that Cora had put out her best china, crystal stemware, and silverware.

Cora came in holding a tray with iced tea glasses. "Katz, I didn't know if you took sugar or not, so it's plain. Sugar is on the table."

"Thanks," Katherine said sweetly.

"Please, everyone sit down. I have baked some amazing appetizers."

Katherine sat down and Jake pushed her chair in. He leaned over and whispered in her ear. "Maybe we should have brought an Erie bib." Katherine and appetizers didn't see eye-to-eye.

Johnny sat down and grabbed four sugar packets. "I like mine sweet, like my wife, Cora," he teased.

Cora flushed. "Oh, quit it, you." Grabbing another tray, she placed a small quiche on each of their plates. "This will hold us over until dinner is ready. I made a pot roast with carrots, potatoes and sweet onions. Jake's favorite."

Jake smiled. "Thanks, Mom. You've really gone all out and everything looks great, but can you sit down for a while?"

Katherine unfolded her napkin and placed it on her lap. "I was just going to mention how lovely everything looks."

Cora sat down and sipped her tea. She abruptly asked, "Have you two set the date? It's important for me to know, because if you want me to book the armory for your reception I'll have to do so right away. There's a huge waiting list!"

"Hold on there, Mom," Jake said. "This isn't a race to the altar." He gently squeezed Katherine's hand.

Katherine was quiet. She didn't know what to say. She wanted to say you're the last person on earth I want to plan my wedding, but she didn't. Her parents raised her to be polite.

Cora continued. "Please, everyone eat. We'll have a salad after this."

It was still light outside. Katherine gazed out the screen window and could see Tommy and Shelly Cokenberger playing badminton in their backyard, while Cokey and Margie weeded their vegetable garden. Margie must have sensed someone was watching her. She glanced over and saw Katherine in the window. She waved; Katherine waved back.

Cora observed. "I don't know why Margie does that. It's simply terrible on the hands. Johnny weeds my garden. Don't you, dear?"

Johnny muttered something under his breath and it didn't seem to be in agreement.

Cora, having a one-track mind, got up and grabbed a large book binder off one of the wicker chairs. "Katz, I'll let you take this home and study it. Maybe we can do lunch and discuss it." She was smiling a toothy grin.

Katherine's eyes widened, then she said, "Yes, I would like to have lunch some day soon. Thank you for inviting me."

After a delicious dinner, Jake made several excuses to leave, and the couple left. Once in the Jeep, Jake said, "Sweet Pea, I'm glad that's over."

Katherine placed the capacious binder behind her seat and laughed. "Oh, it's not as bad as that. The food was delicious. I'm getting used to your mom. I'm relieved she's finally warming up to me."

"Just think of warm thoughts, when you're spending a year researching the book," Jake joked.

"Too bad there's no CliffsNotes to save the day," Katherine teased.

"I bet ten bucks we're married before you finish it," Jake proposed.

"Twenty bucks and we're on." Katherine extended her hand.

Jake shook it. "Deal."

As Katherine hopped out of the Jeep, a loud clap of thunder startled her. Jake joined her, and took the binder from behind the seat. It started pouring down rain.

"Let's get inside before the book melts," Jake advised. "Then we'd be in a heap of trouble."

Katherine softly hummed a few bars of the *Wizard of Oz's* wicked witch theme song, then was glad Jake didn't hear her and figure out that sometimes she thought of his mother as the wicked witch of the Midwest. Well, at least in the state of Indiana.

*     *     *

The overnight storm had blown through quickly, bringing cooler temperatures at last. Katherine grabbed a sweater and trudged through puddles to the library. She had several books to return; she'd gotten addicted to a cozy mystery series and wanted to see if there were anymore. She knew she could go online and buy them, but she liked to get out of the house and catch a breath of fresh air. Since the head librarian, Beatrice Baker, was under house arrest—serving out the rest of her sentence—the staff had changed considerably. The new head librarian was about as friendly as a badger and could out-scowl the best of them. Katherine tried to be friendly with her, but to no avail. The new assistant, who replaced Michelle Pike, was a young

58

man just out of high school, who also completed one of Katherine's advanced computer classes.

Michelle had turned in her resignation in May. She moved to the city to attend summer school at the university. Katherine was proud that Michelle was the first recipient of a scholarship award from the annual Kendall academic fund. It was the first thing on Katherine's list of how to spend her fortune.

Walking back to the pink mansion, Katherine noticed her elderly neighbor, Mrs. Harper, sitting in her wheelchair on her front porch. A new caregiver sat next to her on a plastic lawn chair. Mrs. Harper was in her mid-eighties and lived in an Eastlake-style cottage, complete with ornate gingerbread trim on the gables. The house was built in the 1870s. Recently it was painted a pale blue with white trim. Katherine approved of the new color because it made a pleasant contrast against the pink mansion.

"Hello, Mrs. Harper," Katherine greeted.

"Come up and join us," Mrs. Harper said in a raspy voice. "Katz, the folks in town call me Mrs. Harper because I was a school teacher for many years. My friends call me Birdie. Not that I have many friends left," she transgressed. "Most of them are at the Ethel Cemetery," she laughed, then began coughing. The caregiver handed her a small bottle of water.

Katherine climbed the front steps and looked for a chair, but there wasn't one. She sat on the top corner railing. She wondered about the new name development. She'd known Mrs. Harper, AKA Birdie, for more than a year, and the retired school teacher had never mentioned her given name. Katherine turned her attention to the new caregiver, who bore a striking resemblance to an Erie woman Katherine knew.

"Hello, I'm Elsa Adams." The petite brunette with a bob haircut introduced. She appeared to be in her late twenties.

"I'm pleased to meet you, Elsa. I'm Katz. I live next door."

"Got that part. I've seen you before. Last winter you were at the cake auction, and had that hysterically funny cat that wiped out the cake table."

"My cat, Lilac, and I are banned from returning next year," Katherine said, tongue-in-cheek, then asked, "Are you related to Barbie Sanders? Because you look just like her."

"Why, yes," Elsa laughed. "She's my cousin. Her mom, Aunt June, is my mom's sister. I get told that a lot."

"Barbie was a student of mine." Katherine didn't go into detail about how she gave Barbie private computer lessons because Barbie was so obnoxious in the classroom.

Elsa put her hand up to stifle a laugh. "Knowing Barbie, I bet she was hard to teach."

Katherine wrinkled her nose and then smiled in agreement.

Mrs. Harper said, "Elsa's wonderful. I call her my care angel."

"Ah, that's sweet," Katherine said.

Elsa continued, "I work the nine-to-five shift. I just started a few days ago."

"Do you live in Erie?" Katherine asked, making small talk.

"I rent a room at the Erie Hotel. But originally, I'm from a small town called Peace Lake. It's about twenty miles from here, at the southern tip of Erie County."

"Really?" Katherine asked with interest. "I just rented a vacation cabin close to there."

"Oh, it's a very scenic place. Make sure you go into town, because it's full of antique stores."

"This is good to know."

"Also, there's several really good mom-and-pop restaurants. The food is delicious, but they only take cash. They don't take credit cards."

"Cool. Thanks for the advice."

Birdie chimed in, "I'm also from Peace Lake. I moved to Erie in the 1980s. I inherited this house from my late husband's parents. Have you ever heard the legend of Peace Lake?" Birdie asked.

"No, I don't think I have."

Elsa commented, "It's something tragic that happened before I was born."

Birdie continued. "There's a ghost on the lake."

"A ghost?" Katherine leaned in with interest. "Tell me more."

"In 1968, there was a young man who showed so much promise. He was Peace Lake's high school basketball star. He won a scholarship to go to the university, but was drafted into the army to serve in the Vietnam War." Birdie's voice broke.

Elsa interjected. "Here, ma'am, take a sip of water." She held a small bottle of water to Birdie's lips.

Birdie took a few sips and then carried on with the story. "His high school sweetheart was my daughter, Marcia. They were going to be married, but decided to wait until he got back home. He never returned."

Katherine asked, "What happened to him? Did he die in the war?"

"I'll never forget the day when his family came over and told us he'd died in a terrible explosion. Marcia and I went to his memorial service. Several years went by, and my daughter married and moved to New Mexico. Last month, her husband passed away, so she's moving to Erie to live with me, initially, then she wants to have a ranch house built near Peace Lake."

"I'm sorry to hear her husband passed, but it will be nice for the two of you to live close by. You probably have a lot of catching up to do," Katherine said. "I can't wait to meet her."

Elsa continued her story about the Vietnam soldier, "He never returned, but his spirit did."

Katherine said excitedly, "I love a good ghost story."

Birdie elaborated, "Some people who knew him reported seeing him near the lake. He's as young as his high school picture."

Elsa added, "One witness said he saw him walking out of the lake. He had his army uniform on."

Birdie said to Elsa, "Dear, suddenly I'm very tired. Can we go in so I can lie down for a little bit?"

"Sure," Elsa said, getting up and taking hold of the wheelchair. "Nice meeting you, Katz."

"Nice meeting you, too." Katherine got up and touched Birdie on the shoulder. "We'll talk again. I've got to go home now and feed my cats."

"Bye now," the elderly woman said. "Say hello to the kitties."

# Chapter Four

In the late afternoon, Katherine found a garden shovel in the carriage house and ventured over to the new flower bed. The previous evening, Cokey Cokenberger had brought over his garden tiller and prepared a place in the backyard.

Earlier, Connie London had dropped by ten daylily plants in plastic grocery bags. Connie was in a hurry to meet a friend in the city, so she gave a cursory overview of what Katherine, the non-green thumb, should do. Katherine understood the dig-the-hole part, but was nervous about the planting. Her expertise was limited to taking seeds out of a packet, and on many occasions, that didn't even work for her. Katherine put her foot on the top of the shovel blade and began digging the first hole.

Stevie Sanders, a son of Erie's 'crime boss,' pulled up in his new Chevy Colorado pickup truck. Katherine wondered why he was driving down the service alley when he now lived in the city. Well, at least according to his sister, Barbie. He powered the window down. "Hey, good lookin'," he said. "Fallen off any ladders lately?" Back in October, Stevie had caught her when a rung broke on an old wood ladder in the carriage house. If he hadn't been there, looking for scrap metal, the fall could have caused a serious injury. But that was months ago, and this was mid-summer.

"Hi, Mr. Sanders," Katherine said somewhat formally. She didn't want to give Stevie any hint of interest, considering that the last time they talked he had asked her out to dinner. "How have you been?" she asked cordially.

"Oh, about six-foot-four and a handsome devil. That's what my girlfriends tell me."

Katherine shot a look of annoyance and wondered what he could possibly want. She wished he'd just move on down the road. Instead, Stevie got out of his truck and walked over. Katherine threw one of the plants in the newly dug hole and pretended she knew what she was doing.

"Here, let me help," Stevie suggested. He kneeled down and removed the plant. He added soil from the Miracle-Gro bag and carefully set the daylily back in the hole. Then he began adding soil and patting it around the plant. He didn't talk while he did this. When he finished, he said, "You've got to water it down to git any air pockets out of it."

Katherine smiled. "Thanks. I printed instructions from the Internet, but—"

Stevie interrupted with a smirk on his face. "You're a city girl and ain't never planted a plant before."

Katherine stood up and handed Stevie a towel.

"What do you think of my new truck?" he asked, wiping his hands.

It was then that Katherine noticed the logo painted on the driver-side door: Stevie's Electrical. "I didn't know you were an electrician."

"Yep, got my electrician's license the other day. Learned the basics when I worked for the state; then went to night school at Hoosier Tech."

Katherine knew working for the state meant Stevie's stint with the penitentiary. Curiosity got the better of her and she asked a personal question. "What did you do time for?"

Stevie looked at her for a moment—his blue eyes looked deeply into hers. Then he hung his head and said quietly, "Ma'am, I did somethin' stupid. I drove my buddy to a convenience store for beer, and the dumbass—excuse my language—robbed the place. I've had priors, so I did time for it."

"Hope that guy isn't still your buddy."

"Nope. He can't be," he said, then paused. "Cause he's dead. Went and shot himself down by the river."

Katherine was shocked, but didn't ask any more personal questions.

Stevie fumbled in his pocket and retrieved two business cards. "I stopped by to give you my card."

"But there's two here?"

Stevie ignored the question. "If you ever need an electrician on one of your jobs, please keep me in mind."

"I will," Katherine said. "I'll give these to my project manager."

"One of those is for you," he winked. "Its' got my landline number on it and my cell."

"Okay, thanks," she said dismissively, heading to the house. She thought that was the only way he was going to leave.

"I'm fixin' to go now. I'd still like to take you out to dinner, but my sister tells me you got engaged. I'll respect that."

Katherine held up her left hand and flashed her diamond ring. "Yes, to Jake Cokenberger."

"Yeah, I knew that part. Jake got lucky. Well, keep me in mind. Like I said, if you need any electrical work here at the house, or on one of your projects, I'm your man. Good afternoon, ma'am."

Katherine followed him with her eyes. *What a transformation*, she thought. *Clean cut, well-groomed, tall and handsome. No more unwashed ponytail. I bet he does have a lot of girlfriends, but he's dreaming if he thinks one of them is going to be me.*

The truck was new, and looked like Stevie spent all his free time keeping it clean. It was a perfect shiny black. He tapped the horn when he left. Katherine resumed her gardening when she heard a young voice say, "Hey, Katz, guess what we got?"

Katherine turned to see Margie with her two children, Shelly and Tommy, walking down the alley. "Come over and tell me," she said.

Shelly ran over wearing a Mickey Mouse ears headband. "Daddy's in the dog house."

Katherine thought, *What has Cokey done now? Bad luck seems to follow him around. First the brief affair with a murderer, then being accused of the murder of Robbie Brentwood.*

Margie said to Shelly in a scolding voice, "Young lady, explain to Ms. Katz what you just meant."

Shelly giggled her signature cackle and said, "Daddy's building a dog house. We got a new puppy."

"That's wonderful. What kind did you get?"

Tommy answered, "A yellow lab. We named him Oscar."

"Congratulations!" Katherine offered, then to Margie, "What does Spitfire think of the new puppy?"

"Well, kiddo, Oscar isn't a puppy, but Shelly calls him one anyway. He's a rescue from the shelter. His foster mom said he was great with cats, so we adopted him. And do you know what?"

"Oh, no! Don't tell me," Katherine said hesitantly. "Are the two of them not getting along?"

"Not at first, but I think they've arranged some sort of truce. Oscar stays out of Spitty's way, and vice versa."

"That's cool! I want to see him. I want to pet him."

"He's assisting Cokey with the grill right now. We'll bring him over some time."

Tommy picked up the shovel. "Can I dig, Ms. Katz? Please, I wanna dig."

"By all means. Go for it," Katherine laughed, handing him the shovel. "I need nine more holes."

"Nine?" Tommy scrunched up his face. He started to dig while Shelly supervised.

"What did that Sanders boy want?" Margie asked nosily.

Katherine was used to Margie's frank questions. "He has his own business now. He's an electrician. He stopped by to find out if I had any work."

"Oh, lordy. Not one of the Sanders. They'd steal you blind—"

"How?" Katherine interrupted.

"Well, for starters, taking off with the construction equipment after the job is finished. Stealing copper tubing and pipe is a big thing now, or air compressors, nail guns, you name it, then selling it on the black market."

"Really? Indiana has a black market?" Katherine asked skeptically. "You think Stevie Sanders would do that?"

"I wouldn't trust anyone who did time for theft. He robbed a convenience store. On that sour note, I'll leave ya now. Kids, come on. We're walkin' to the gas station for fountain drinks. Cokey's grilling hotdogs in a minute. Katz, want to come over and join us?"

"Oh, thanks, Margie, but Jake's coming soon. We're doing something else."

Margie winked. "Gotcha."

"When are Cokey and you taking the kids to Disney World?"

Margie said happily. "Soon! I'm countin' the days. We're leavin' on Wednesday."

Shelly jumped up and down. "I'm never taking my ears off. I can't wait to meet Mickey."

Katherine said, "When you do, I want a pic of it."

Margie nodded and said to her twelve-year-old son, "Tommy put down the shovel and come on. I can't carry four biggie drinks by myself."

Shelly giggled and skipped ahead. Tommy sullenly put down the shovel. "See ya, Katz," he said shyly. "Say 'hi' to the cats. Two head pats for the one who flies."

Katherine knew exactly what he meant. "I'll give Lilac a chin scratch, too."

*     *     *

The following morning, Katherine walked outside to water the daylilies she and Jake had planted the evening before. She scratched at the multitude of mosquito bites she'd gotten and lamented at not using the bug spray as Jake had suggested.

Her cell rang, so she reached in her Capri pants' pocket. It was Barbie Sanders—former student—now a busy career woman with two Siamese kittens named Dewey and Crow.

"Katz, how are ya?" Barbie began amicably.

"Fine. How's school?"

"I'm taking the summer off from classes. I'm working full-time at a vet clinic. Today's my day off. I've got a minor problem-o."

"What's that?" Katherine asked, wondering why Barbie would be calling with a problem when she was so sure of herself.

"It's the kittens."

"They're okay, right?" Katherine asked, concerned.

"Yeah, they're okay, but I'm not. They're driving me crazy. They keep me up all night with their playing. They're constantly under my feet. They're very demanding . . ."

Katherine held the cell to her ear and finished watering the plants. "Kittens are always like that. When Iris was a baby, she was the most hyperactive cat I've ever seen. Give them time. They'll settle down."

"Well," Barbie said, then hesitated. "I was wondering if I could bring them for playtime with your cats. Maybe the kittens need adult cats to teach them manners."

"Sure. Let's schedule a time to do that," Katherine answered.

"How about now?"

"Now? Where are you?"

"Oh, ha! Ha! I'm parked in front of your house."

Katherine laughed. "I'll be right there." She pressed the End button and put the cell back into her pocket. Walking to the front of the house, she watched Barbie get out of a new red Mustang. A premonition hit her in the head like a ton of bricks. She thought about Carol Lombard and the last time she'd seen her. Carol had been driving a new red Mustang.

Barbie flipped the front passenger seat and pulled out a cat carrier. Katherine rushed over to help. Sitting calmly inside were two of the most adorable, long, lean and slinky seal-point Siamese boys. Their bodies were a light cream color with seal masks that hadn't darkened yet. Their slanted eyes were a dark blue and slightly crossed. One of them belted an explosive, loud, "Mao," while the other one yawned.

"They're so cute . . . I can't take it," Katherine gushed.

"Thanks, Katz," Barbie grinned ear-to-ear.

"They've really grown. How old are they now?"

"A little over eight months. It's hard to tell them apart, so I put collars on them. Red is Dewey, and black is Crowie."

"Ah, you call him Crowie. Sweet. Come, bring them inside." Katherine grabbed one end of the carrier and led the way.

Inside, Scout and Abra sat on the parlor windowsill, looking apprehensively at a cat carrier being brought into the pink mansion. This could only mean one of two things: either a short trip to the vet, or a long road trip in the car. They jumped off the windowsill to officially greet Katherine and Barbie at the door.

Katherine used her cell phone to tap in the code to disable the house alarm. "Okay, now we can go in," she said, opening the door.

Barbie asked, "You set the alarm when you're just outside?"

"Pretty much."

The two walked into the atrium and set the carrier down. Dewey and Crowie were very interested and ventured closer to the front of the cage. Scout and Abra began circling the carrier while Iris sat stoic, peering in with curious, blue eyes.

Lilac and Abby dove off their parlor valance perch and came in, as well. They began circling the carrier in the opposite direction as Scout and Abra. Finally, getting dizzy from the activity, Lilac and Abby hopped on top and began pawing the outside of the cage. The kittens didn't make a sound. Curiously, the other cats didn't, either.

Barbie kneeled down on the floor. "When do you think it's safe to open the door?" she asked.

Katherine pondered, "I've always thought it best to make introductions slowly, but the kittens look rather sedate. My cats just had breakfast, so they should be pretty sleepy and want to take a nap."

Barbie laughed her signature, but subdued laugh. "Oh, ha! Ha! What's the worst thing that could happen?" She slowly opened the door.

Scout and Abra quickly moved to the front of the carrier and stood like prison guards on either side of the cage's open door. Lilac and Abby craned their necks to lean over and look inside. Iris made the first move. She sauntered over, sniffed briefly, and licked one of the kittens on the head.

Katherine cooed, "Ahhh, Iris, my sweet girl. Barbie, I don't think we have anything to worry—" She didn't have time to finish her sentence. The kittens wiggled their rumps and shot out like cannon balls with the five adult cats in hot pursuit. The kittens were flying—leaping over furniture, dodging underneath tables, springing off walls. They fled to the living room, which displayed the most expensive antiques.

On top of a mirrored chest of drawers, a Tiffany lamp careened. Barbie screamed, "Katz, grab that lamp."

Katherine ran to the chest and rescued the lamp. "Barbie, look out behind you!"

The kittens vaulted to the five-shelf display stand that displayed Katherine's great aunt's Lladro porcelain collection. They did a dead stop, and then used their back legs to launch off the bottom shelf. The display stand began to wobble as if the town of Erie had been struck by an earthquake. The figurines began swaying, teetering, close to falling and being smashed to smithereens. The kittens shot out of the room. The adult cats were getting tired of the chase; Lilac and Abby bowed out and assumed their regular positions on top of the window valance.

"No. . . no. . . no," Barbie scolded, sprinting to the stand. She began catching the figurines that were tumbling off the shelves. She handled them like a professional juggler and managed to return them to their original places without any damage.

Scout, Abra and Iris galloped after the kittens as they thundered upstairs. Each cat tried to out-paw the other. Katherine and Barbie heard a loud crash.

"Oh, no, Barbie! We'd better get up there to make sure none of them is hurt."

It was too late for a sprint up the stairs. The three cats and two kittens had returned and were now heading for the back office.

Katherine joined the chase and called back to Barbie, "Close the door behind me."

Barbie couldn't move fast enough. The race shifted and the cats galloped back upstairs.

Returning to the atrium, Katherine said, "Hopefully the kittens will discover the new playroom up there."

Barbie asked, "Playroom?"

"I converted one of the guest rooms into a cat room. It's a cat's dream come true."

"I want to see it," Barbie said excitedly.

The two climbed the stairs and found the kittens busy in the playroom. They'd discovered a stash of busy balls and were batting them around the room.

"What did I tell ya?" Katherine said knowingly.

"This is way too cool," Barbie said in awe.

The playroom was in the front of the house on the east side. In the curved turret area, Margie had designed padded benches underneath each of the three windows, so the cats could soak up the morning rays. In the center of the room were five multi-leveled cat trees. Cokey had built a two-level cat walk around the room. He made it out of reinforced plywood and then carpeted it. The first level was four feet from the floor, while the second level was eight feet. Various ramps made of sisal provided access to the walks. The crowning point was two beams that intersected the middle of the room. This had become Lilac's and Abby's favorite feature.

"I asked Cokey to take the Victorian furniture out of here and store it in the attic," Katherine explained.

"You said guest room. Where's your guest gonna sleep? Oh, ha! Ha! I get it—in the attic?"

The kittens discovered the first cat walk and were streaking around the room. The adult cats were trying to catch their breath. They hadn't had this kind of exercise in quite some time.

Katherine laughed, "No, not the attic. I have a guest house on Alexander Street where my *future* guests will stay." Katherine didn't elaborate that the room had been Colleen's mum's while she was staying last winter. As much as she loved Colleen's mother, when mum visited in the future, she'd be staying at the guest house.

"Well, Barbie," Katherine continued, "That was what I call a Siamese stampede. I think they're going to be okay. Let's go back downstairs. Hey, do you want something to drink? Soda, iced tea, or iced something else?"

"Sure," Barbie said, then to the kittens, "Mommy will be back in a minute. Have fun!" The kittens totally ignored her. Scout, Abra and Iris assumed their positions on top of the cat trees with a look of pure delight on their brown masks.

Before Barbie left the room, she walked over and petted Iris. "How's my sweet baby?" she asked. Iris reached up to be held. Barbie was no stranger to Iris. Many months before, she had saved the Siamese from harm's way. Barbie picked up the purring cat and gently hugged her. Iris gently nipped her on the ear.

"Ouch, I forgot you do that," Barbie said. She placed Iris back on the cat tree and joined Katherine in the hallway. "I just love that little girl the same way I love Dewey and Crowie."

Katherine answered. "It's funny how they pull your heart strings."

They walked downstairs to the kitchen. Barbie was talking a mile a minute about her job, her school, and her new boyfriend.

Katherine stopped at the mention of boyfriend. "A boyfriend? Good show. What's his name? Is he from Erie?"

"Get me somethin' to drink first. I'm dyin' of thirst." Barbie headed for the kitchen table and flopped down on one of the Parsons chairs. "Oh, somethin' diet. I'm tryin' to lose weight for my new designer jeans I just bought. I'm down to a size fourteen."

Katherine rummaged in the refrigerator and found a Diet Coke. She popped the tab and moved to get a glass.

"Oh, I'll take it straight up, if you please," Barbie said.

Katherine handed her the can. "So, what kind of diet are you on?"

"It's a custom-diet made just for me. There's a retired pharmacist who lives out in the country and he makes me these delicious milkshakes. They're full of vitamins, minerals and all of that good kind of stuff. He prepares enough for the week so I pick them up, put them in my cooler, and take them home. I drink them for lunch."

"What do you eat the rest of the time?" Katherine asked curiously.

"For breakfast, I eat a light meal and for supper, I eat a balanced meal. Lots of veggies and about four ounces of meat—chicken, beef or pork. He's got it all written up for me. I'd recommend him to you, but Katz, I think you are *way* too skinny."

"Barbie," Katherine said, shocked. "I'm not skinny."

"Oh, ha! Ha!" Barbie laughed. "I'm sorry. You know how I sometimes I blurt out things without thinkin'."

Katherine glared at her. "My doctor says I'm a healthy weight."

"Oh, don't get your feathers ruffled up. I was just kidding." Barbie winked.

"Tell me about the new boyfriend." Katherine gladly changed the subject.

"He's from France. His name is Henri DuPree. I met him in one of my classes, but he didn't ask me out right away. The other night, I went clubbin' with a bunch of friends and ran into him. We ended up dancing all night."

Katherine smiled. "I hope he's a cat lover. What do the kittens think of him? Do they love his French accent?"

Barbie's face lit up like a Christmas tree. "Tonight is our first date. Henri is taking me to dinner at a fancy schmancy restaurant in the city." Barbie continued smiling, then became serious. "Well, back to the kittens, what do you suggest I do about Dewey's and Crowie's bad behavior?"

"You haven't told me what the bad behavior is. I can see they're hyperactive, but that's normal for the Siamese breed."

"They both have a habit of jumping on me and climbing me like a tree. It wasn't bad in the winter when I wore jeans, but I've been wearing shorts. Look at my legs." Barbie had several deep scratches on the backs of her legs.

"I'm certainly not an expert. I just learned the ropes by being owned by cats," Katherine began. "When my cats are really bad, I put them in the powder room for time out until they settle down. Do you have a place like that in your apartment?"

"Yep, I have a second bedroom. After seeing your cat room, I'm kinda thinkin' about makin' it into one. I never have guests or sleepovers. But when I do, he sleeps in my room." Barbie covered her mouth. "Did I just say that?"

Katherine giggled and continued with her cat advice. "Buy a spray bottle. Fill it up with water. When they do something bad, say the word 'no' and spray them."

Barbie rolled her eyes in exasperation. "I tried that. The terror twins knocked the bottle out of my hand. Later they hid it. They're super smart."

"Forgive me for laughing," Katherine chuckled. "I would have loved to have seen that. Iris and Abby hide things in an old chair, but a water bottle might not fit."

"My kittens hide stuff under my bed." Barbie glanced at her watch. "Oh, it's getting late. I've got to go." Barbie got up. "Thanks for the pop. I'll just take it with me."

Katherine smiled. "I guess we should find the cats."

As they headed to the atrium, Dewey was fast asleep inside the carrier, but Crowie was missing. Barbie quietly closed the gate. She began calling the kitten's name. "Okay, where's my Crowie? Crowie, where are you?"

Barbie climbed up the stairs and was almost to the top when Katherine said, "Crowie's down here."

Barbie headed back. "Where?"

"Up there!" Katherine pointed.

On top of the parlor window valance were Lilac and Abby with Crowie in the middle. They were fast asleep.

"Oh, ha! Ha! Sweet! Listen, Katz, I've got a million errands to run. Then I've got to get back to the city for my hair appointment. Gotta look good for the date, right?"

"It's awfully hot outside. Do you want to leave them here, and then pick them up on your way out of town? It's no trouble."

"Katz, you're a doll! Thanks a bunch. I shouldn't be but a couple of hours."

"No problem. When you come back, give me a heads up call and I'll have your kittens ready to go."

Barbie blew a kiss at the carrier and grabbed her capacious Coach bag. She rushed to the front door. "See ya in a little while," she said, leaving.

"Okay. Bye." Katherine simultaneously reset the house alarm and looked out the door sidelight, watching Barbie get in her car and leave. She then walked to the parlor.

"Lilac, Abby," she said softly to the exhausted felines. "Can you get Crowie to come down?"

"Chirp," Abby cried sleepily and put her paw over her eye.

"Me-yowl," Lilac belted.

The kitten woke up, yawned, and stretched to full height. Without warning, he dove off the valance and landed in Katherine's arms.

Startled, Katherine said, "You little monkey." She cradled the kitten and kissed him several times on the head. "You've got to warn me when you're going to do that." She placed him inside the carrier with his brother Dewey, who woke up for a split second, then went back to sleep. Katherine walked to the linen closet outside the powder room to find a soft fleece baby blanket for their bedding. She was surprised Barbie didn't have a blanket already in there.

She wondered about Barbie's drinking the nutrition shakes. Why would anyone drive all the way to the country just to get them? Why would a retired pharmacist make a diet shake in the first place? Was there a drug in it? Something was fishy. Katherine didn't want Barbie to revert back to her old, wild days.

*　　　*　　　*

In the parlor, the antique grandfather clock bonged six times. Dewey and Crowie stood on their hind legs with their paws on the clock cabinet, watching the large pendulum move back and forth. They moved their heads like they were following a tennis match. Their person hadn't returned.

Katherine was beside herself with worry. She walked back to the office and rummaged through a stack of business cards on her desk until she found the one Stevie Sanders had given to her. She entered his number on her cell.

Stevie answered, "Stevie's Electrical."

Katherine didn't mince words. "This is Katz Kendall. I'm worried about your sister, Barbie."

"How can I help ya, ma'am?"

"Barbie came over this morning, left her kittens, and said she'd return in two hours. That was nine hours ago."

"Left her kittens? What kittens?" he asked, flustered. "I wouldn't worry none. My sis is never on time.

She'll roll up soon. By the way, did she say where she was goin'?"

"She said she had a bunch of errands to do. One of them was to go out in the country."

"I'm sorry, I didn't catch what you just said. I'm driving to the city. Sometimes I lose calls in this area."

"She said she was running errands," Katherine repeated.

"Well, if she's this late, she must have driven out-of-state to do them," Stevie laughed nervously. "Listen, I'm losing the signal . . ." The call ended.

Katherine was going to hang up anyway. Stevie was absolutely no help. She questioned why she called him in the first place. Maybe brother and sister weren't that close. Why else wouldn't he know about Barbie's pride and joy—her kittens?

While she was on the phone, Jake disabled the house alarm with his cell and came in. "Hey, Sweet Pea.

Where's those demon kittens you've been texting me about?" "Mao," Dewey yelped, rushing in to meet the newcomer. Crowie followed close behind. Jake sat down cross-legged on the floor. The kittens immediately started climbing him like a tree. "Ouch," he said, then to Katherine, "We need to trim their claws. I take it Barbie hasn't come back."

"Not yet. I just called her brother, Stevie. He said this was her MO to be late."

"Where's the other cats?" Jake flipped Crowie on his back and began kneading the back of his neck.

"They're probably sacked out in the play room. The kittens are like the Energizer Bunny. They've worn out my cats." Katherine moved to the parlor window for the fiftieth time and looked up and down Lincoln Street. No red Mustang. No Barbie.

"Have you been looking out the window all day? You're going to wear out the carpet. Maybe Barbie had car trouble."

"In a new vehicle? I don't think so. She would have called me."

"Ooh, that tickles," Jake said to Dewey who was tunneling inside his polo shirt. "Sorry, Katz, what did you just say?"

"That Barbie drives a new car. You wouldn't expect it to break down."

"Maybe she ran out of gas."

"I hope not. She said one of her errands was in the country."

Jake added, "If she did have car trouble, she's got a huge family network of kin to help her."

"She was so happy when she left here. She was happier than I've ever seen her."

Jake extracted the kitten from his shirt. "Katz, I know how much you try to see the best in people, but Barbie has a reputation in Erie. The only way she can live it down is to move, which she has done."

"What does that mean?" Katherine asked sharply.

"Her dad's a criminal; her brothers have done time. Barbie has done time and once ran a whore house. That's why the locals call her the massage queen."

"Yes, I know that, but I think the whore house was just a rumor—a nasty Erie rumor—started by the ball-cap gossips down at the diner. Just because she lived in a rundown trailer on the bad side of town doesn't make her a criminal."

Jake put his arms in the air defensively. "Just sayin'."

"She had a hair appointment in the city, which she missed. She told me she was having a first date with a man she really liked. She wouldn't just take off and leave her kittens. She loves these cats!"

Jake stood up. Dewey launched off an Eastlake chair, and was hanging on the back of his belt while Crowie climbed up his jeans and perched on his shoulder. "Hey, you guys." He pulled Crowie off his shoulder. "Katz, his collar's a bit tight."

"Barbie put them on to tell them apart, but I think it's obvious who they are. Dewey's mask is darker and he's bigger than Crowie."

Jake didn't hesitate. He removed Crowie's collar and began rubbing the kitten's neck. "Poor little man," he said softly. Dewey trotted over and Jake removed his as well.

"I tried to take them off, but the kittens wouldn't stand still long enough for me to remove them. You must have the magic touch."

Jake winked.

"Katz, I don't want to sound like an alarmist, but maybe you should call the police."

Katherine found the chief's number in her contact list and pressed the number. The call went directly to voice mail. She explained the situation and voiced her concerns. When finished, she called Stevie, but he didn't pick up. A message popped up on her screen, "Out of area."

The chief was still at the station when he returned the call. His tone was serious. "Hey, Katz. I know I shouldn't be divulging this private information, but I can count on you to be discreet. I've been in contact with Barbie's brother, Dave. He came down to the station. He was concerned because Barbie was supposed to meet him at noon and she didn't show up. In light of the message you left me, I convinced Dave to file a missing person report."

"Oh, no, Chief. A missing person report . . ."

"In Erie, if there's a suspicion of foul play, it's our policy to not wait twenty-four hours so I sent email to every Tom, Dick and Harry in the Indiana law enforcement world. I won't bog you down with the official channels I contacted, so I'll come right to the point. Brace yourself."

"Okay, hit me with your best shot."

"Barbie's car was found at a closed rest stop outside Shermanville. In case you don't know, that's about thirty-five miles south of Chicago. The officers didn't find Barbie, but did find blood on the back seat—a lot of blood. We may be looking at a homicide."

Katherine gasped. The room began to spin. She thought she was going to faint. She held onto the edge of the marble-top curio cabinet for balance. "Oh, no . . .," she cried. Jake rushed over and put his arm around her.

"An investigating team is working on this," the chief continued. "Right about now they're probably combing the vehicle for clues as to what happened. Shermanville police have a search and rescue team looking for Barbie."

"This is terrible." Katherine paused, then asked, "Chief, don't state-operated rest stops have surveillance cameras?"

"Good point, but like I said, this rest stop is closed to the public. I've been told that the only way to enter it is to drive by the entrance, which is blocked, then back up via the exit lane. The rest stop building itself doesn't exist anymore. There probably hasn't been a working surveillance camera in years."

"Did anyone see her drive in?" Katherine asked hopefully.

"No eye witnesses. As soon as we punched in Barbie's license plate on the official database, a Shermanville officer found the car. The keys were still in the ignition."

"Where is she then? I can't see Barbie walking away from her new car unless she was coerced," Katherine said. "Maybe someone abducted her, but why?"

"Don't know, but the Chief of Police is keeping me up-to-date. Katz, got another call coming in. I'll keep you posted." The chief hung up.

Katherine placed her cell on the cabinet. She wrapped her arms around Jake and buried her face in his chest. "Barbie's car was found outside of Chicago. There's blood on the back seat. It might be Barbie's. Jake, I'm afraid that something horrible has happened to her."

"Shhh," Jake whispered in Katherine's ear. "It sounds bad, but we don't know. Let's just take it one step at a time."

Dewey and Crowie had returned to the room and were taking turns climbing the legs of Jake's jeans. He picked both of them up and held them against him. "I'm staying here tonight, Katz. I don't want to leave you alone, and these kittens look like they need some TLC."

"Why do you say that?" Katherine said, wiping a tear from her eye.

"Because as much as you think Barbie walks on water, these cats seem a bit scrawny to me. Crowie looks like his ribs are poking out."

"I noticed that. They're almost nine-months-old and should be heavier. I know Lilac and Iris were at that age."

"They look malnourished."

"In case you didn't know, the modern, wedge-head Siamese are lean, but . . ." She didn't finish her sentence. She thought about Barbie making a comment that *she* was too skinny. Now Barbie might be dead.

"I think we need to go to the kitchen and feed them. It's supper time for the cats." Jake said the words to get Katherine's mind off the terrible news.

"Okay, sounds like a plan. Let's feed them," she said wearily. "If Barbie doesn't turn up by tomorrow, I'll take them to Dr. Sonny for a check-up."

"It wouldn't hurt."

Following Jake through the back office, Katherine noticed her computer monitor was on. It should have been in sleep mode. She hadn't used the computer in hours.

"Oh, no," she said under her breath, fearing some awful news the cats had surfed up.

Jake had already gone to the kitchen and was busy feeding the noisy cats—all seven of them.

"Be there in a second," she called to him in the next room. She hurried over to read the screen. She hoped there was an easy explanation, such as the kittens had learned to walk across the keyboard. If it was Barbie-related, she didn't want Jake to see it. She wasn't in the mood to talk about her cats' special talents, although she suspected he probably already knew.

On the screen, was the first page of an Indiana spirit-hunting website. It showed a Photoshopped rendition—clearly not an actual photo—of a handsome man dressed in a Vietnam-era military uniform, walking out of a foggy lake.

"Peace Lake," Katherine muttered; the hair on the back of her neck rose. *This is too much of a coincidence to be one of the cats walking across the keyboard. Why would they surf to this page? Does this have anything to do with Barbie?* She questioned.

Jake called from the kitchen, "Hey, you two, get back here and eat."

Scout and Abra darted into the office. When they caught Katherine's attention, they began to sniff the air like they smelled something unpleasant that she wasn't aware of. Then, they started swaying back-and-forth in unison. Scout's pupils became mere slits, while Abra's were dilated and staring wide-open. Scout arched her back and hissed. Abra shrieked; foam was forming on the side of her jaw. They began hopping up and down like frightened Halloween cats.

Jake ran in and saw the two agitated felines. "Katz, what's wrong with them? Did they get into any poison or something?" He rushed over to them. Scout emitted a menacing growl.

Katherine shook her head and said loudly, "Cadabra, no. Stop it!"

Scout fell on her side and was breathing rapidly. Abra began furiously washing Scout's face. "Raw," she cried.

Jake was shocked and backed away from the cats. "What's wrong with them?"

"They're shocked by something they see in the future," she said in a matter-of-fact voice.

Jake walked over to Katherine and put his hands on her shoulders. "Why on earth would you say such a thing? We don't know that."

"Scout and Abra will be fine in a few minutes. I've seen them do this before. They only do the dance when something terrible is about to happen, or may have already happened. I have a strong suspicion that Barbie's in a great deal of danger."

"Whoa, your cats are psychic?" Jake asked skeptically. "This is over-the-top, Katz. When did this happen before?"

Katherine hesitated, then said, "When I found Vivian Marston's body. Scout did the swaying back and forth in front of Chief London. The afternoon you were shot, Scout and Abra did the same thing by Patricia Marston's body."

"Strange," Jake remarked. "When you called Scout 'Cadabra,' that was like launching a word bomb. She stopped immediately."

"'Cadabra' was Scout's stage name. She doesn't like to be called that."

Scout got up and hurried over to Jake. She rubbed her face on his knee and reached up to be held. Jake picked her up, "You really hurt my feelings when you growled at me. It's time to calm down now. Your heart is racing a mile a minute." Jake began pacing the floor with Scout in his arms. "It's okay, baby doll. Just calm down."

Katherine returned her attention to the computer screen. "Jake, I have something to tell you."

"What is it? You're fifty shades of pale."

"I'm not going to Savannah with you."

Jake set Scout down. "Why not? We've got our flights and hotel lined up. My mom and dad are coming over to take care of the cats."

"I meant to tell you earlier but —"

Jake broke in, "Katz, are you worried about leaving the cats? They're in good hands."

Katherine shook her head. She exited out of the website without having to explain it to Jake. She'd already divulged enough about the cats.

Jake continued. "Is it because Barbie's missing? The police will find out what happened. You don't need to sit at home waiting for a phone call. The chief can call you in Savannah."

"It's got nothing to do with Barbie."

"Katz, I was really looking forward to this trip with you. Everyone in the history department is attending. Professor Watson is taking Leslie." Jake moved a chair over to Katherine's. He sat down dejectedly. "My paper is about prohibition in Erie and your great Uncle. I wanted you to be there when I presented it."

"I'm so sorry. I decided not to go before Barbie went missing. I talked it over with my grief counselor and she agreed I need some alone time."

Jake got up and pulled Katherine out of her chair and into an embrace. "Is everything okay with us?" He kissed her on the forehead.

Katherine hugged him back. "Yes, everything is fine."

"What are you going to do while I'm away?"

"Remember that cabin near Peace Lake—the one with the stocked pond? I've rented it for four days. I'll be leaving the same day you fly out."

"Are you taking the cats with you?"

At the mention of cats, seven inquisitive felines circled the couple, yowling loudly.

Scout cried a loud "waugh" to Katherine, which sounded like "you better take us."

Katherine said to the cats, "Alone time doesn't include you. Elsa will take good care of you."

"Naugh," Scout protested.

"Elsa? Who's Elsa? I thought my parents were the official cat sitters."

"Elsa is the caregiver next door. She'll be taking care of the cats and staying at the pink mansion while I'm away."

"Katz, wouldn't you rather have my parents—whom you know—take care of them, instead of someone you hardly know?"

"Elsa has a side business—pet sitting in the Erie area. She's licensed in the State of Indiana—bonded and insured. I did an Internet search. Her references check out just fine."

"What's Elsa's last name?" Jake inquired.

"Adams. She's Barbie Sanders' cousin. Elsa's mom is Barbie's mom's sister. So they're related on the maternal side. Barbie's mom was Sam Sanders' third wife; she lives in Kentucky now."

"Interesting," Jake said.

Katherine replied optimistically, "I figure when Barbie comes back, she'll be pleasantly surprised to see her cousin taking care of all the cats. I think it's too much to ask your parents to care for seven feisty felines, especially since I'm not going with you. Now I've got to figure out how to tell your mom."

"I'll tell her. She'll have a million questions, but I can handle it."

"So, let me wipe that frown off your face." Katherine took Jake's face in her hands and kissed him on the lips.

# Chapter Five

Katherine stood in the atrium and said good-bye to the cats for the tenth time. She was apprehensive about leaving them with a total stranger, but felt confident that Elsa would take good care of them. She couldn't help but worry a little. *What if Elsa disarms the security system and a nutcase gets in? What if there's a home invasion and someone steals one of the cats like when Iris was catnapped?*

"Katz, they'll be fine," Elsa assured. Not only was she a pro at handling cats and dogs, but also their worried owners. "I've got my list of instructions. I'll come here in the morning. When I'm finished pampering your cats, I'll be next door taking care of Mrs. Harper. When Tara relieves me at five, I'll return and stay overnight. I've got the phone numbers of whom to contact in case I need help, but I'm a great predictor of things. Everything will be okay." She picked up Abby and held the purring

Abyssinian in her arms. It was a rare sight to see Abby on the floor because she preferred high places.

Katherine wished Elsa hadn't said the part about being a great predictor of things, and hoped that didn't jinx her four-day trip to the cabin.

Katherine reached down for her last bag when her cell rang. Glancing at the incoming call screen, she answered, "Hi, Jake! Wow, your flight must have gotten in early."

"Twenty minutes. I'm waiting in the taxi stand for a ride to the hotel. If you think Indiana is hot right now, you should be here in Savannah. It's as hot as Hades. What's the cabin like?"

"I haven't gotten there yet. I'm still at the pink mansion."

"Katz, it's getting late. Plus, I just watched the weather channel while I was picking up my luggage.

Indiana is supposed to have some powerful storms rolling through. You better get going."

"Actually, I'm leaving now. I don't like the prospect of storms, but I think I can get to the cabin by seven or so. Elsa gave me a shortcut because she has a client who lives out there."

Jake advised, "I love ya, but you've got an awful sense of direction. I don't want Elsa's directions to get you lost out in the middle of nowhere, especially in this heat. Katz, just use the GPS."

"Oh, I have an awful sense of direction," Katherine repeated. "Maybe I should take my compass." She became serious and said, "I'm glad you got there okay. I love you. See ya Sunday."

"Ditto," Jake said ending the call.

Elsa advised, "Katz, one thing I should mention. The cell reception out in that neck of the woods is terrible."

"Not to worry. I don't plan on calling anyone." Katherine reached down for her duffle bag and noticed that Abra had crawled on top of it. "Raw," the Siamese cried with sad eyes.

"It's okay, sweet girl. You've got to move now. Mommy will see you Sunday."

Scout ran to the front door and collapsed against it. She began shrieking a loud string of sharp protests. Elsa moved to pick up the Siamese, but Scout bared her fangs and hissed.

Undaunted by the display, Elsa reached down for Scout. "What's upsetting my little cupcake?"

Scout reared on her hind legs and scratched the pet sitter.

"Scout, stop that," Katherine scolded; then to Elsa, "I'm so sorry. Come with me to the kitchen. I've got a first aid kit in one of the cabinets."

Elsa said, "I'll take care of it in a minute." She reached down for Scout again, but the angry Siamese dove for Katherine and dug her claws in Katherine's jeans.

"Ouch! That' hurts. Quit it! Scout, let go."

Abra collapsed on Katherine's shoe and wouldn't budge. "Raw," she screeched.

Katherine hesitated for a moment, then reached for the door handle. Scout lunged for the door, stood up on her hind legs and grasped the door handle with both paws. Abra hopped back on the duffle bag and lodged her claws in the canvas.

Elsa tried to grab Scout, but Scout cried a menacing, deep throaty growl.

Katherine sighed, "Elsa, there's been a change of plans. I'm taking Scout and Abra with me. I can't leave them when they're clearly in a delirious state."

"Ma-waugh," Scout agreed.

"Shouldn't we call the vet?" Elsa asked, concerned.

"No, this is something my two sealy girls do," Katherine explained. "Just help me get them in their carrier and load them in the car. I've got to gather a few extra things. Then I really need to get going before it gets dark."

"Okay, I can do that. Lilac, Abby, Iris and the little ones will be just fine. Don't worry."

"Thanks. I really appreciate it."

*     *     *

Once on the road, Katherine spoke to the cats, which were sitting inside their carrier atop the folded back seat. "That was the best performance I've ever seen. You two deserve the Academy Award."

Scout and Abra answered by thumping their tails inside the carrier. Thumpity thump thump.

The feminine GPS voice droned, "Turn left on Highway 41 and follow the highlighted route."

"Waugh," Scout protested. Something about the GPS lady's voice irritated the sensitive Siamese. Finally,

Scout stopped objecting, and the two sisters settled down. When Katherine looked in her rearview mirror to check on them, Abra had her paw draped over Scout's back. Katherine was thankful they had finally gone to sleep.

On the front passenger seat was the map Elsa had drawn, as well as the computer printout directions to the cabin from the owner, Leonard Townsend. Townsend's email instructed Katherine to drive to his house first, which was less than a mile from the cabin, and pick up the key. He explained that he didn't have a telephone or cell phone, and that he drove to Peace Lake's library to use one of their computers. He advised that if she needed an answer to email, she'd have to wait twenty-four hours.

Initially, this lack of communication worried Katherine, but then she thought maybe he was frugal. Although she had been apprehensive, she felt more at ease when she remembered the five-star reviews from satisfied vacationers. Also, she had packed her own five-star protection—her Glock.

*　　*　　*

It was a quarter to seven when the rain started. At first it was a light, steady rain, then it turned into a torrential downpour. The windshield wipers could barely keep up. Katherine leaned forward in her seat and clutched the steering wheel. "I've got to find someplace to pull off," she said, squinting.

"Waugh," Scout cried, waking up. The pounding rain on the Subaru's roof woke up Abra, as well.

"It's okay. We'll be there in a minute. Go back to sleep," she said in a calm voice. Katherine saw a sign for Ox Bow Trails and quickly pulled into the parking lot. She parked, then yanked her cell out of her bag. Elsa answered right away.

"Wow, I guess I was wrong about the cell reception. What do you think of the cabin?" the pet sitter asked.

"Elsa, I'm not there yet. I'm so lost. I've been following the GPS directions. I think I've gone too far."

"What was the last thing you passed?"

"I'm in the Ox Bow Trails parking lot. The place is desolate. Not a person or vehicle in sight."

"Okay, you've gone way too far. Turn around and go back about fifteen miles. When you see a sign for Port Logan, turn left. Do you still have my directions?"

"Yes, I do," she said guiltily, embarrassed about not following them in the first place.

"Once you get to Port Logan, follow my instructions. Okay?"

"The rain is so hard. I think I'll sit here a minute until it lets up. Thanks, Elsa."

"You betcha."

Katherine disconnected the call and re-read Elsa's directions. She committed them to memory. When the rain let up, she pulled back onto the highway and drove the fifteen miles. The cats became quiet again, which was a relief, because Katherine swore she was a nervous wreck, and kicked herself for wanting to have this little adventure in the first place. She just wanted a few days to chill out about the wedding—AKA Cora's show—and the fact that Jake was insisting they have a prenuptial. On the latter issue, Katherine knew there were good legal reasons for it—Scott Wilson had said so. She reasoned, *Jake wants the prenup so he can show me he's not marrying me for my money.*

Turning onto Port Logan road, Katherine drove five miles to a fork in the road. She veered right. She left a paved road for a dirt one. It had a lot of potholes, which woke up the cats. "Raw," Abra protested.

"I think we're about there," Katherine consoled.

The narrow dirt road meandered through a wooded area, then turned into a private lane that led to Leonard Townsend's house. The house was a gingerbread-trimmed farmhouse, which had seen better days. Katherine parked in front and wondered where Mr. Townsend's car was, and why the place seemed so desolate. No porch light. No lights inside the house.

"I'll be back in a minute," she said to the Siamese. "Gotta get the key." Katherine climbed out of the SUV and was relieved it had stopped raining. She could hear distant thunder. Perhaps the storm wasn't over yet.

Both cats were standing tall in the carrier, very curious about their surroundings.

Katherine walked up to the front porch. When she knocked on the battered screen door, a manila envelope fell on the threshold. She picked it up. The word "key" was written in bold, black letters. She opened it and pulled out a handwritten note with a map to the cabin. Leonard apologized for not being there, and wrote that he had to leave to tend a sick friend. He said he'd be back in the morning. Katherine extracted the key and got back in the car.

She worried, *How many people have keys to the cabin? What if there's an ax murderer lurking or a zombie in the barn?*

"Should we go home?" Katherine asked the Siamese.

Scout nudged the metal gate; Abra cried a sweet "raw."

"Okay, I take that as a no. We'll have our back-to-nature adventure." She turned the key in the ignition and pulled out. The road to the cabin was just as bumpy, but not quite as hilly. It had gotten dark early because of the rain, so Katherine turned on her headlights. Driving around a sharp curve, she could see the faint outline of a cabin. A flash of lightning further illuminated it.

"I love it!" Katherine exclaimed. It looked better than the Internet picture; it appeared brand-new. She parked in back, got out, and explained to the cats, "I'm going to leave you out here for a moment. I've got to go in and cat-proof. Let me unload your litterbox first." She grabbed a large litter pan, bag of cat litter, and two water bowls.

Unlocking the cabin door, she found the light switch and turned it on. She also found the porch light and flipped on that one, as well.

"It smells wonderful in here. Like a pine forest," she said out loud. Looking around, she could see new construction. The walls were natural wood paneling, the floors a rustic-looking oak. The kitchenette had new appliances; a flat screen TV sat on the fireplace mantel. Upstairs were two bedrooms and a small bathroom; the downstairs had two bedrooms and a luxury bathroom, complete with soaking tub. Katherine picked a room for the Siamese and placed their litter pan in there. The screened-in porch seemed dry, and when she brought in the cats, she put them out there while she unloaded the rest of the car.

Once the car was unloaded, she picked up her cell to call Jake. There was no reception. "I was afraid of this.

Oh well. I wanted to get away, so I'm truly getting away," she mused.

Katherine opened the door to the screen porch, and Scout and Abra shot into the cabin's main room. They immediately explored every nook and cranny.

"I bet you're hungry," Katherine called after the cats. "I'll feed you after you've settled down. Want to help me make the bed?"

The Siamese ignored her. Instead they found a wide windowsill and were sitting back-to-back like bookends, peering outside. Scout's tail was twitching; Abra's was thumping back and forth.

"At-at-at-at-at!" Scout clucked.

"What are you two looking at?" Katherine pulled the partially opened curtain and looked outside. A large crow was standing on top of the Subaru. "That's the biggest bird I've ever seen," Katherine said, astonished.

The bird sensed a human and flew away, emitting a loud string of "caws."

"That, my little furry friends, was a bird. Not one of your Manhattan pigeons you used to watch on the window ledge, but a crow. Crows have their own language and can even count. What do you think about that, Abra?" she asked, petting her on the head.

Abra glanced back at Katherine and cried, "Caw."

Katherine laughed. "Did you just say caw?"

"Raw," Abra answered.

"Okay, enough. I've got to make up my bed if we're going to get any sleep tonight." Katherine moved to the bedroom and found an antique armoire. Inside were clean bed linens, blankets and enough towels to last a month. The king-sized bed had a log headboard and footboard. When Katherine looked up, she gasped. Mounted above the bed, close to the ceiling, was a giant faux moose head with a large rack of antlers.

Curious about what their human was doing, the Siamese trotted in, took one excited look at the moose head, and effortlessly leapt to the top of it. The moose head was so large, they could both sit on it, balancing between the ears and the antlers.

"Good thing I didn't bring Lilac and Abby or you wouldn't be sitting up there now." Scout and Abra were down-to-earth cats, while Lilac and Abby were more comfortable being able to survey life below.

After several hours of unpacking, feeding the Siamese, and eating her own dinner, Katherine curled up on a sofa, which looked like it came straight from a rustic decor catalog. The frame was made from logs and the green cushions had a bear and elk scene printed on them. All of the cabin furniture seemed to be constructed out of logs. The TV console had hand-hewn log legs with a bear on each of the two cabinet doors. Inside was a row of DVDs of some recent-release movies. Katherine wasn't sure if she'd watch any, because her goal was to be at one with nature.

The small dining table consisted of a plank top on log legs, with benches on either side.

The thunderstorm pushed through a much-needed cold front, so Katherine turned on the gas log insert in the fireplace. Scout and Abra trotted into the room, and flopped down on their sides. Scout washed Abra's ears, then Abra returned the favor. This peaceful interlude lasted about half a minute until Scout bit Abra's neck, and the two went flying from room-to-room in a fast chase.

Before Katherine and the cats retired for the evening, she made sure the windows were locked, as well as the front and back doors. She latched the door to the screened-in porch. She'd wished that it had been a regular door, because she feared someone could easily cut the screen and gain entry. In her bedroom, she leaned a security bar against the door. She looked out the back window, amazed at how dark it was. Even with the porch light on, she couldn't see beyond her SUV.

Once she hit the bed, she fell fast asleep, but was awakened by two hyperactive Siamese who wanted in. Finally, after two minutes of their plaintive cries and the constant jiggling of the door handle, she got up and opened the door to her brown-masked pests, who flew in. She went into the second bedroom, and brought back their litterbox.

She said to the rambunctious Siamese, "Okay, you're sleeping with me, but whatever you do, do *not* spend the night jumping up and down from that moose head."

Abra innocently squeezed her eyes and instantly sprang to the moose head. Scout muttered something, and then joined her. Katherine tugged the blanket over her head. "Go to sleep!"

In the middle of the night, a loud clap of thunder startled Katherine out of a deep slumber. A flash of lightning revealed two Siamese looking intently at something outside the window.

"Is it the crow again?" she asked sleepily.

Scout turned and cried a mournful "waugh." It sounded like a warning.

"What's out there?" she asked uneasily. Getting out of bed, she dragged herself to the window and pulled the curtain aside. Another lightning stroke briefly illuminated the backyard. A tall, broad-shouldered, heavy-set man was standing at the edge of the woods. On his head he wore something black that covered his face. *Or did he have a face?* She wondered.

Katherine stood back, her heart beating fast. "What the hell? Who is that?" Heavy rain pelted the window glass. The wind picked up and whipped around the cabin.

Abra cried a deep, menacing growl. Scout hissed and hit the window glass with her paw. Katherine said to the cats, "Get down. Let me check again." She walked back to the window and looked out.

At first her eyes focused on the rivulets of rain running down the glass. With the next flash of lightning, the man was now standing right outside. He wore a black motorcycle helmet, and the visor was up, revealing a deformed face with one eye missing. Katherine screamed and fell back. She scrambled to turn the night light off, so the man couldn't see her.

Scout and Abra—still growling and hissing—ran underneath the bed. Finding her Glock, Katherine cautiously moved to the side of the window and peered out. The man had vanished. She panicked, *Where is he? What if he gets inside?*

Katherine closed the curtain and whispered to the cats, "It's okay. We're going to stay in here and not leave this room until morning."

"Ma-waugh," Scout agreed.

She sat down on a cushioned chair and tensely waited out the rest of the evening—flinching at the slightest sound outside. It was only at the morning's first light that she fell asleep, and then slept for hours. It was noon by the time she woke up.

"Scout. Abra. Where are you?" she called, looking around for the cats. "Why did you let me go to sleep?" The Siamese were back up on the windowsill.

"Tap, tap, tap." Something outside tapped on the glass.

"Oh, no. Not again," Katherine said fearfully. "Get down, girls." When the cats wouldn't budge, she snatched both of them and set them on the floor. Then she slowly drew the curtain aside to gaze into the dark quizzical eyes of a crow. She leaped back. "That's it," she announced anxiously. Reaching down, she picked up both cats. Kissing them on the head, she said, "We're going home."

The cats ignored her and wiggled eagerly to be set free. She put them on the floor. Then they jumped back onto the windowsill. "At-at-at-at-at," Scout chattered to the bird.

"Tap, tap, tap." The crow "cawed" and flew away.

"Here's the plan. I'll get dressed and reload the car." She opened the door to the combo living room/kitchen and did a quick glance around the room. Everything was exactly the same as she'd left it the night before. Returning to the bedroom, she hurriedly put on jeans and a tank top, then laced up her sneakers. Putting the Glock in her waistband holster, she left the cabin, closing the door behind her. She scanned the area, searching for the man who might be ready to attack her. Scout and Abra remained on the windowsill and followed her with their eyes.

Katherine trudged in the mud to the edge of the woods where she had first seen the man the previous night. She saw footprints—large boot prints—where someone walked out of the clearing to the Subaru, then to the cabin. The hair on the back of her neck rose.

*I've got to get out of here*, she thought. Briskly entering the cabin, she was surprised to see Scout and Abra waiting inside their carrier. They quivered against each other.

"I know you're scared, but we're leaving—now." She grabbed her bag and found the car keys. Picking up the cat carrier, she rushed to the car. Scout cried softly.

"I'll have Chief London come back, or someone from the police force help me get the rest of our stuff. We're not staying here another minute." She opened the back hatch of the Subaru and placed the carrier inside. Rushing to the driver's seat, she climbed in and took off too fast, skidding in the mud. Slowing down, she drove out of the muck and proceeded to the owner's house. Pulling in the drive, she noticed a beat-up, blue pickup truck parked there.

*That must be the owner's*, she assumed. "I'll be right back, my treasures," Katherine said to the cats. "Gotta return the key." Before getting out of the SUV, she studied the yard and house. Once she was sure the coast was clear, she walked to the front porch.

Curiously, the door was ajar. She knocked twice, then peered in. "Mr. Townsend?" she called. "It's Katz Kendall." No one answered, so she walked into the house. She was surprised to see a coffee table covered with a mound of pill bottles. She picked up one and examined it. Inside was a thirty day supply of Oxycodone. The label named a pharmacy she'd never heard of. Picking up several more, she found each bottle labeled the same. *Oh, my God,* she panicked. *These can't belong to one man. Leonard Townsend must be a drug dealer.*

Running to the front door, Katherine tripped on a throw rug and came down hard on her knees. Getting up, she was startled to hear the loud crack of a gunshot from the back of the house. Slowly moving to the next room, Katherine looked out the kitchen window. A man was standing over a prone body; she surmised the body was Mr. Townsend's. The standing man looked up and saw her.

"Run!" she yelled to herself. Katherine fled from the house and raced to her car. Getting in, she quickly turned on the ignition. She looked over her shoulder to see if the cats were okay. It was then she realized the cat carrier was missing.

"What the hell is happening? Why would anyone steal my cats? I've got to get to a place with reception so I can call the police." Backing up, she nearly ran into a tree, then skidded down the lane in the direction of the main highway.

She hadn't gone far when the beat-up blue pickup raced up beside her. The man inside wore dark glasses and a red ball-cap turned backwards. He honked the horn and motioned for her to pull over. The lane was so narrow, she could hardly keep her vehicle on the road. "Pull over," the man yelled out the window. "I just wanna to talk to you."

Katherine slowed down and hoped the man would pass her. When she turned her gaze back to the road, she saw a woman dart out from behind a tree. Katherine tried to avoid her; the Subaru hit a rut in the lane and went airborne. The SUV flipped upside-down and skidded down the lane, coming to a stop in a shallow drainage ditch.

She felt the airbags deploy, exploding into her chest and side. Up ahead, the driver of the blue pickup came to an abrupt stop, then backed up. It was then Katherine heard someone in the woods, firing at the pickup.

Hanging upside down and still secured by her seatbelt, she pushed the partially deflated airbag out of the way and peered through the Subaru's window at the pickup. She could see that one bullet had hit the truck's back window, where a large spider-web crack had formed. Another bullet had glanced off the passenger-side mirror. That was enough for the driver; he sped off. Katherine remained conscious for a few more seconds. Then everything went dark.

# Chapter Six

Elsa sat in the pink mansion's formal living room on a wingback chair with Iris, Dewey and Crowie. Iris was curled up on her lap, and the kittens were nestled in her arms. They were watching the original version of *Cat People*. Elsa was a movie buff and loved Katherine's collection of old movies. When her cell rang the *Dukes of Hazzard* theme song, Iris leapt off her lap. Dewey and Crow climbed to the top of the chair.

"Dang, where's the remote? Which one of you little thieves stole it?"

The cell continued ringing. She answered it at a yell. "Elsa speaking! Hang on. I can't hear. I need to turn the DVD player off." Rushing to the DVD player, Elsa turned it off manually, and got back on the phone. "I'm sorry. Who's calling?"

Jake asked hurriedly, "Have you heard from Katz?"

"Why, no," Elsa replied. "I talked to her last night. Her GPS had gotten her lost, so she called me for directions to the cabin. I gave them to her. Why?"

"I haven't heard from her, which is very unsettling. I've tried to contact her, but my texts come back undelivered."

Elsa offered, "The cell reception out there is *terrible*."

Iris yowled into the phone loudly—almost urgently.

"Are you at the mansion?"

"Yes, Mrs. Harper's daughter is in town and took Birdie to the city. I got the day off."

"How's the cats?"

"Just fine, but Scout and Abra put up such a fuss that Katz took them with her. I think the other cats are spoiling me, because—"

Jake interrupted, surprised. "Scout and Abra are with her?"

"When she tried to leave, they pitched a royal catfit. I've never seen anything like it—foaming at the mouth, practically."

"Elsa, I've got to hang up now. Catch you later." Jake disconnected the call and immediately punched in Chief London's cell phone number.

The Chief answered in his usual grumpy way, "Yeah?" he barked.

"Chief London, this is Jake. I'm in Savannah at a conference, and Katz is renting a vacation cabin south of Erie. I fear that something has happened to her."

"And why is that?" the chief asked.

"The last time I spoke to her was late yesterday afternoon. I haven't heard from her since. My calls and texts have gone undelivered."

The chief leaned back in his chair and put his feet up on his desk. "Maybe there's a logical explanation for this—Katz forgot her phone. Maybe it needs to be charged. Maybe *your* service plan doesn't cover the boonies."

"I know it's not my cell, because my Dad has gotten my text messages. Elsa Adams said Katz called her last night to tell her she was almost at the cabin. Elsa hasn't heard from her since. Katz would be calling to check on her cats. Something's not right."

"Yeah, you've got a point there. Who's this Elsa person?"

"She's the new caregiver for Katz's neighbor, Mrs. Harper. I hate to bother you, but can you check into this? I've got the address of the rental."

"Sure, it's not like I'm doin' a crime scene today. Fire away." The chief removed the cap from his pen and began writing on his desk pad.

"The cabin is near the town of Peace Lake, but it's not on the lake. It's located several miles north, on a pond."

"Who owns it?"

"A Leonard Townsend."

"What did you say?" The chief's voice now showed signs of concern.

"Leonard Townsend. Why?"

"Leonard Townsend owns a big tract of land . . ." the chief paused, then added worriedly, "He used to live in Erie. He's got a big-time criminal record. I've arrested him many times."

Jake gasped. "Katz rented a cabin from this man."

"The crimes are drug-related. He does an alternative medicine business from his house, but he doesn't work with herbs, exactly. Recently, Sheriff Johnson busted him for growing marijuana on his land."

Jake said, "My talk is at three p.m. I've changed my ticket to get in at eight tonight. I should be in Erie by ten. I'm going to drive out there and pray she's alright. By the way, did you find out what happened to Barbie Sanders?"

"Nope, still missing. Okay, listen to me, Jake. Don't be driving out there at night. The place is remote. You'll never find it. I'm off tomorrow. I can drive you there, if you want."

"Okay. Appreciate it," Jake said.

"In the meantime, I'll call Sheriff Johnson and see if he can send a cruiser out to the cabin and check on Katz. I'll talk to you later."

"Thanks." After he hung up, he thought, *No, I'm going there tonight.* He called Elsa again.

When she answered, he said, "I'm worried about Katz. What do you know about this Leonard Townsend person—the man who owns the cabin? You drew Katz a map. How did you know where he lived?" he asked suspiciously.

Elsa began cautiously, surprised by Jake's accusing tone. "I was caregiver for a woman who lived near him. She knew him because he bought herbs off of her. You see, he's into holistic medicine."

Jake almost spit it out, but didn't say, *Yeah, marijuana.* "Elsa, would you text me the directions to Townsend's house—the same route you gave to Katz?"

"Sure. No problem."

"Thanks so much. I'm going to drive to the cabin from the airport. I was supposed to meet Katz there Sunday. I'll just show up tonight," Jake laughed, deliberately seeming to make light of the situation, because he didn't want to concern or upset Elsa.

"Oh, she'll be so excited to see you," Elsa giggled.

"Okay, great. Listen I have to go. My talk is in a few. Thanks for your help." Jake hung up and nervously ran his hand through his hair. He was worried. He remembered Scout's and Abra's bizarre dance. He remembered how Katz had said it was their way of communicating something bad was going to happen. He prayed it had nothing to do with Katz or her cats.

## Chapter Seven

Stevie Sanders parked in front of the Dew Drop Inn tavern on the outskirts of Erie. His father, Sam Sanders, owned the place, but Sam rarely frequented it since he'd moved to Chicago to live with his new love interest—a woman half his age. Stevie walked in to find Eddie Muncie, the bartender, waiting for him.

The bartender whispered, "Hey, you better get your cuz home. He's drunker than drunk, and he's tellin' an awful story. Git what I mean?"

Stevie knew the bartender for many years and understood the urgency. He walked directly to the table where his cousin Jimmy was talking animatedly to two other men. They were laughing at some kind of big joke. Jimmy didn't notice Stevie and kept talking, slurring his words.

"Yeah, you should have seen that bitch when I ran her off the road," he bragged.

"Hey, Jimmy. Long time no see. What's happenin', Cuz?" Stevie asked.

Jimmy laughed some more, but the other two men looked sheepish. They got up and moved to a different table.

"Drinks all around," Stevie instructed the bartender. Then to Jimmy, he asked, "What ya talkin' about. Sounds like my kind of story."

"It's like this Stevie, my man, ole man Townsend has met his maker, if you catch my drift. He was demandin' more of a cut, so I offed him."

"Really? Did my old man approve that? I hope for your sake that you covered your tracks. You got rid of the body, right?"

Jimmy ignored the questions and kept on laughing. "I'm gittin' to that, but here's the funny part . . . "

Bartender Eddie brought two beers and set them down, then he took care of the two other men.

Stevie took a long drink. "I want to hear it. Had a crappy day dealin' with customers who don't want to pay."

Jimmy gulped down four big swallows. "Seems ole Townsend had a woman friend. Some babe with short black hair. Drove one of those newer model Subarus."

Stevie cringed but didn't let Jimmy know he suspected the woman was Katherine Kendall. She matched the description. Most women in Erie wore their hair long. Katherine's hair was short, and she drove a newer model Subaru.

Jimmy continued, "When I found out Townsend was trying to screw us, I took him out back and had a little conversation. His stupid woman was standin' there, lookin' out the window. She saw what happened, so I had to get rid of her."

"Right," Stevie agreed. "She's a witness."

"Yeah, but here's the funny part. She flew out of there like a house on fire, and I chased her down. She can't drive for shit. My truck hardly touched her vehicle. She hit something and it flipped big-time. Horrible wreck. She's *dead*, man. We got nothin' to worry about."

"Yeah, sounds cool to me. Finish your beer, buddy. Gotta git ya home. Don't want any of those probation fellers comin' around and seein' you drunk."

Leaving the bar, Jimmy noticed Stevie's new truck. "Movin' up in the world, big shot."

Stevie answered, getting in, "Hey, don't get sick in my truck or they'll be hell to pay."

Jimmy snickered, "I ain't drunk."

The ride to the Sanders' Trailer Court was a few minutes away from the bar. As soon as Stevie helped Jimmy into his trailer, he advised, "Get some sleep. I'll talk to ya later."

"Yeah, Cuz."

Walking back to his truck, Stevie pulled out his cell phone and called his father. They spoke in code, just in case any lawman was listening.

Stevie began, "Hey, Dad. My girlfriend's sick with the flu."

"That's too bad," Sam said. "Seems odd the flu would be goin' around now in the middle of summer. How bad is it?"

"Oh, enough to take her to the ER. Just callin' to let ya know."

Sam feigned a laugh. "Well, son, you can at least tell me who it is."

"Jeanne."

"That's too bad. Take care of your woman. I'll be home soon."

"Thanks, Dad." Stevie hung up.

The conversation had been innocent enough. Jeanne was the code name for Jimmy. Sick with the flu meant Jimmy had done a stupid thing that could expose all of them. Take care of your woman simply meant Sam Sanders would make sure Jimmy was out of the picture— permanently. But it also meant there couldn't be any witnesses.

Stevie hoped the woman wasn't Katherine. He thought angrily, *Just when my life is changing for the better, that idiot Jimmy totally screwed things up.* Stevie pounded his steering wheel several times, then fired up the engine. He drove a little faster than necessary, but no cops were in sight to pull him over. He had to get to Townsend's place before the law did. Hell, it was so far in the sticks, he didn't think that was likely, but he had to get the Oxy for his father . . . and also had to find Katherine.

*What if she was dead like Jimmy said?* He wondered. He was sad for a moment, then focused on what he had to do. First and foremost, he had to make sure the

Oxy was safe. He feared the wrath of his father more than any law enforcement agent.

He had to clean up the crime scene, then bury poor old Leonard. Where to bury him, he didn't have a clue— someplace on the property. Only when the burial was done would he make an anonymous call to the Erie County Sheriff. He'd use the untraceable burner cell phone he kept just in case of an emergency. He'd call in the accident. If he didn't, he knew no one would find Katherine on Townsend's property. He started ticking off the reasons. First, Townsend's tract of land covered four hundred acres. Second, the private lane to the house was off the beaten track. The only people turning on Townsend's road were lost vacationers, occasional cabin renters, and drug dealers.

*But what if I find Katherine alive*, Stevie pondered. *Should I just make up some lame excuse why I'm in that neck of the woods?* Yeah, he'd do that. He'd have to gain her confidence to find out what she knew.

*    *    *

Katherine moaned as the man loaded her in his ATV's utility trailer. "You're hurting me." She caught a glimpse; he wore a black motorcycle helmet. *The same man from last night,* she panicked. *The stranger in the woods.*

He threw a blanket over her, then mounted his three-wheeler.

The pain in her ribs was so intense, Katherine blacked out again.

The man drove slowly through the woods on a narrow path. He tried to reduce the rugged ride for the injured passenger in the back. When he came to a clearing, he pulled into the cabin's parking space, where Katherine had parked her SUV the night before. He turned off the ATV, walked to the cabin door, and kicked it open. Then he returned for Katherine. He scooped her up in his arms and carried her to the bedroom, gently laying her down. Katherine gave out a cry of pain, but didn't wake up.

The crow flew in the opened door and perched on the footboard, gazing with wonder at the motionless woman.

The man grunted to the bird.

The crow understood. "Caw," the bird acknowledged.

Katherine stirred for a second and mumbled, "My cats . . ."

The man nodded, left the room, and went back outside. He climbed on his ATV, drove into the woods, and turned into a path to Townsend's backyard. There he loaded up his dead friend and took him a half-mile to an abandoned cemetery. The last tombstone read 1889. He stopped for a second to read it. "Lester Townsend. Born 1840. Beloved husband and father. *One of his relatives, no doubt*, he thought. He'd have to leave the body here and then go back to the house to get the right tools to bury him.

He liked the old man, who was always just "Lenny" to him. He was kind. He didn't treat him like he was some kind of freak. Lenny let him live off his land. Every week he'd leave him supplies. There were rundown cabins everywhere. Lenny said he could live wherever he wanted, but that he should move around a lot. That way, no one from the outside would find him. Lenny said it was their secret, and that he'd take it to his grave. In return for Leonard's act of kindness, the man in the woods would take care of the property and the cabin rental—sight unseen. The big man sighed, *I didn't think he'd die today.*

Starting up the ATV, he headed back to the house. He worried about the tracks he was leaving in the mud, but he didn't have time to cover them up—too many tracks, not enough time. He trudged through the mud to a side shed and opened the door. That's where he'd taken the cat carrier. He looked inside at the two Siamese and wanted to comfort them, but they hissed and moved to the back of the cage.

He liked cats and took care of the strays in the woods. He took care of all God's creatures—those in need, or those that were just hungry. Gazing at these cats, he sensed they were special—intelligent-looking. He knew the cats were Siamese. Long ago, he'd seen Siamese cats on TV. The smaller one blinked at him; the man winked back with his remaining eye.

He took a moment to catch his breath. He tried to piece together what happened less than an hour ago. The night before, he didn't know anyone was staying at the cabin, because Lenny didn't leave him a note. When he saw the Subaru, he checked things out in case a squatter had moved in. This had happened before, and the ending wasn't a happy event for the squatter. He didn't mean to frighten the woman who looked out the window, so he left for his own cabin and stayed there until the following morning.

When he got up, he drove his ATV over to Lenny's, but he didn't approach the house because of the blue pickup. He suspected a drug deal was going on, and he didn't want to be a part of it. He left the ATV in the woods and sneaked behind the shed to get a closer look at the backyard. He was close enough to see Lenny standing in the yard with a short, muscular guy. They were joking about something. The short man was cackling loudly. He didn't know the short stranger; he'd never seen him before.

When the young woman with the short black hair pulled up and parked, he got distracted and moved to get a closer look. He followed her with his remaining eye, then realized she was the woman staying in the cabin. Her car windows were down, and he could hear cats meowing inside.

This was the part of the story that puzzled him. Did the shooting happen before the woman walked into the house, or afterwards? He remembered hearing the gun shots and wanting to warn the woman to get out of there. He knew that for her safety, he had to get her into the woods. But he didn't want any harm to come to the cats, so he opened the Subaru's hatchback and took out the carrier.

He ran it over to the closest shed and placed it inside. He was thankful the cats had stopped screeching. This guaranteed the killer wouldn't find and harm them.

Looking over his shoulder, he saw Lenny's body. It looked like he'd been shot in the head. He remembered sprinting to his ATV to get his rifle. He was a crack shot. He hoped he could get back to the woman before the short man did, but he was too late. She was already in her SUV, racing down the lane.

He was squinting through the rifle sight, aiming for the blue pickup, when he caught movement behind a large oak tree. It was that woman he'd sighted for several days. Who was she? Where had she been hiding? She made a wild dash to the edge of the woods and seemed to be trying to catch up to the Subaru. She was limping. He lunged after her—stopping only to take a few shots at the blue pickup; the first round shattered the back window. When he heard the terrible crash, he prayed it was the pickup, but it wasn't.

The woman in the woods saw him—saw his disfigured face—and screamed. She staggered deeper into the woods. He had to find her, but first he had to take care of the cats.

Securing the cat carrier in his trailer with a bungee cord, he reached for his rifle and stepped cautiously to the house. He prayed the strange woman with the wild blond hair wasn't inside, and if she was, he hoped she didn't have a gun. He didn't think she did because, she'd had the opportunity to shoot him several times when they encountered each other in the woods. *Better be safe than sorry*, he thought. It was getting very hot outside. He didn't want to leave the cats outside too long.

Jogging to the house, he opened the screen door, which opened noisily on its rusted hinges. He checked out the house, then walked back to the living room coffee table full of Oxy. He found a black shopping bag nearby and swept the drugs into it. He'd deal with that later. He didn't want Oxy. He wanted something else.

He moved to the kitchen pantry and lifted a plastic box off one of its shelves. It was Leonard's medical emergency kit. Removing a glass ampoule and several syringes, he carefully put them in his pocket and walked back to the ATV.

When he arrived at the cabin, the crow flew out of the house and landed on the cat carrier. "Caw. Caw," the bird cried.

"Caw," the smaller Siamese answered. The bigger one stared at him suspiciously; she bared her teeth and growled.

He freed the carrier from the bungee cord, then carried it to the cabin. He set it down on the bedroom floor.

Katherine lay on the bed, deep in sleep. The man inspected her body to see how significant the injuries were. She had several contusions on her face and head. The palms of her hands were bruised, as well. When he lifted up her tank top, he found a very large hematoma had formed on her chest and ribs. He surmised that the SUV's frontal air bag did a number on her. She was small, petite. She was probably sitting too close to the steering wheel. There wasn't much he could do about the bruised ribs.

She didn't appear to have any broken bones. He prayed she didn't have internal injuries, because then he couldn't help her. All he could do now was give her something for the pain. If she awakened by the next morning, he'd figure out what to do then.

He was sure about one thing. He wasn't going to seek outside help for two reasons: One—that short drug dealer was bound to come back and get the Oxy. Two—he was not giving up his location to the authorities. He'd get rid of the dealer first, and worry about the second later.

"Waugh," the larger Siamese cried.

The man grunted. He opened the carrier gate, but the two cats stayed inside and refused to come out. That was okay. He needed to give the woman something for pain, and he didn't want them in the way.

He reached inside his camouflaged shirt and pulled out a syringe. He needed to inject the drug in her hip. He gently rolled her on her side. She moaned in pain. From his back pocket, he pulled out his folding hunter's knife and cut a slit in her jeans. He then used several alcohol pads to sterilize his hands.

Tearing the plastic wrapper off the syringe, he stuck it in the glass ampoule, measured the required dose of morphine, and stuck the needle in her hip. She was so petite, he was afraid to give her much. The narcotic would help ease her pain. She needed to sleep to heal her injuries. He moved her back on her back and vowed to check on her later. He couldn't stay with her. He had too many fish to fry before he'd come back.

When the man left the room and closed the door, Scout and Abra leapt out. They cautiously circled the room, then jumped on the bed. Abra began licking Katherine's face. Scout stood tall and paced back-and-forth at the end of the bed, waiting to do ferocious battle with anyone who tried to hurt Katherine. She loved her human as much as she did her sister, her littermate Abra. Although the man from the woods smelled terrible, Scout sensed he was trying to help them. It was the other man the Siamese had to worry about.

# Chapter Eight

Katherine thought she heard Abra whisper something in her ear. The cat's whiskers tickled when she brushed against her face. But cats can't talk, Katherine rationalized.

She lapsed into a dream about an event that happened in another place and time—before she rescued Abra from the cruel magician. Scout and Abra had been stage performers in the Catskills, working for Harry's Hocus-Pocus act, before Katherine provided their forever home. Now an image nagged at her subconscious, something about when Abra was stolen. *But I wasn't there*, Katherine thought. *No one knows what happened to Abra but Abra herself.*

"I can tell you," the cat said. "Raw."

The cat's voice in the dream trailed off. Katherine woke up and glanced around the room. She weakly tried to get up, but felt as if iron weights were holding her down. It was night, and the room was pitch-dark. She could hear the cicadas' keening whine rise, subside, and then fall silent. She heard a movement in the far corner—a rustling sound. Then a shape slowly approached the bed. A giant crow landed and perched on the footboard. It shrieked, "Caw!"

*I must be out of my mind,* Katherine thought. *I'm dead or dying. I hurt all over. What's happening to me?* She heard a distorted grumbling. It was a hoarse male voice.

Katherine opened her eyes for a split second, then quickly closed them. The huge man was standing, leaning over, looking at her. His face was terribly disfigured. The entire left side of his face was a mass of scars; his left eye was missing. She cringed and tried to move.

He mumbled something and then held a bottle of water to her lips. She took several sips and wanted more, but he took it away from her.

"Want Jake," she managed to say, before lapsing

into another dream.

# Chapter Nine

Stevie Sanders turned into the lane that led to Townsend's house, rounded a curve, and nearly hit a disheveled woman limping toward him. She was flailing her arms wildly. He jammed on the brakes and the woman collapsed in front of his truck.

Getting out, Stevie rushed over to the woman and then stood back, surprised. "Damn, sis. What are you doin' out here?"

Barbie sat up. "Thanks for askin' if I was okay. What are *you* doin' out here? Whatever the reason, I don't care. I just want you to take me out of this hell hole and get me to the nearest McDonalds. I'm starvin' to death."

Stevie helped her up. "Let's get you in the truck."

"I can hardly walk," she said, taking his hand. "I twisted my ankle."

Stevie helped her up to the running board, then pushed her into her seat.

"Ouch," she cried, then, "Got any water?"

"Yeah," Stevie said, moving to his toolbox in the back. He pulled out a bottle of water. "Here," he said, handing it to her.

Stevie climbed into his seat and started the engine. "Listen, I've got to pick up something I left at the house."

"What?" Barbie shrieked. "Are you insane? We ain't goin' to Leonard's house."

"It will just take a minute."

"You can't get back there. Katz wrecked her car; it's blocking the road."

"Is she dead?"

"Is she dead?" she repeated incredulously. "What you should have asked is 'What's she doin' out here?'"

"Okay, fine," he said, throwing his hands up in the air, irritated. "What are you doin' here? You're a freakin' missing person. Dave went down and filled out the paperwork. The law is looking for you all over the country."

"I drove out here Tuesday to get my diet shakes."

"What?" Stevie asked skeptically.

"Leonard makes me diet shakes. When I got here, he met me at the door and said his car was in the shop and asked me to take him to town. I said okay. We both went in the house and I paid him for the shakes. Then we're just about ready to leave the house when *your* yahoo cousin, Jimmy—"

Stevie interrupted, "Was anyone else with him?"

"Ahhh, no," she said arrogantly. "But the way Jimmy was carrying on, it sounded like there was. He was so drunk, or high on something."

"Well, hurry up with your yammerin'. Finish the story. We need to git goin'."

"Leonard got rough with me and yanked my bag off my shoulder—my damn Coach bag that cost me a fortune.

He took my bag and my keys! Then he tells me to hide in the closet. He goes outside and then I heard shouting. I'm peekin' out the window and see Leonard and Jimmy get into a fight. Jimmy stuck him with a knife. Then he threw Leonard into the back seat of my *brand new car* and took off."

"Why didn't you try and walk to get help? It ain't that far to walk to the main drag."

"In these shoes?" she answered. "If you didn't notice, they've got a three-inch heel."

Stevie shook his head. "Barbie, why do you wear those freakin' shoes in the country?"

"I waited a few minutes, then ran out to Jimmy's truck. I thought the numbnut would have left the keys in the ignition, but no dice. I searched everywhere in his truck. Coming back to the house, I tripped on a root and hurt my ankle. So, brother, that's pretty much it. I've been hidin' out, waitin' for them to get back so I could figure out a way to get my car back. What day is it anyway?"

"Friday."

"Oh, my lord! I've been out here three days!"

"You said Katz had a wreck. Is she dead?"

"No, but it's bizarre that she shows up here in the first place. Nobody knew I was coming out here, so if she was looking for me, how would she have known?"

Stevie started to get out of the truck, but Barbie gripped his arm. "Don't go out there without a gun. There's a freakin' crazy man who lives in the woods. He'll shoot you dead."

"You're out of your mind."

"After Katz had her wreck, he pried her out of the vehicle and took her—God knows where. He's a huge man, built like the Hulk. His face is horrible. It's all scarred up and he doesn't have an eye. Katz showed up, goes inside, then next thing I know—"

"You're not makin' any sense. How can she show up when the Hulk has her?"

"Dang it! This was right before the accident," she said, frustrated. "Katz went inside Leonard's house for a few minutes. I heard two gunshots. Then she runs out and gets in her car. Jimmy races from the backyard, jumps in his piece of crap truck, and chases her. Now I'm gettin' tired of tellin' this story, so give me your dang cell phone so we can call this in, but first let's get the hell out of here. We can't get a signal here."

Stevie got out of the truck and reached behind his seat. He grabbed a flashlight and a gun. "Goin' to the house. Got to git something. You wait here."

"No, get back here, you dumbass. That nut case will shoot us if we don't get out of here."

# Chapter Ten

Katherine opened her eyes and saw Abby the Abyssinian sitting beside her. She had a busy ball clenched in her jaw and dropped it on the bed. "Chirp," the cat cried, then said in English, "I know something about your great aunt."

Katherine closed her eyes. When she opened them again, Abby was gone. "I'm going insane," she said. She lapsed into another dream.

The estate attorney, Mark Dunn, was helping her great aunt Orvenia get into his green Honda. Mark said, "We've got to get a move on if we're going to make it to Wisconsin. The breeder said there was some kind of *Taste of Chic*ago festival going on, and the traffic may be horrendous. That might delay us, so I figure if we leave now, we can avoid the rush."

"You just jinxed it," Orvenia said in a croaky voice. The elderly woman smiled and climbed onto the passenger seat.

Katherine struggled to wake up. "But I say that! Why would my great aunt say the same thing I'd say? I learned that from Colleen, and she's from Ireland, not from Indiana." She nodded off again.

Mark fired up the engine and peeled out onto Lincoln Street. "You look very dapper today," he said.

"Thank you! I buy my clothes online now. Beats having my chauffeur drive me into the city."

*Nuts*, Katherine thought. *My great aunt wasn't up on technology. The only thing she had that was modern was the small flat screen TV in the atrium. She didn't even own a computer.*

"So, Miss Orvenia," Mark said affectionately. "How did you find out about this breeder? And why an Abyssinian?"

"I saw this picture of a ruddy Abyssinian in a magazine. I read the advertisement for the breeder in Wisconsin and gave her a call. These cats seem so exotic to me. I've had Siamese all my life, but . . ."

*Wait a minute?* Katherine asked. *Did she just say Siamese?*

"I thought the kitten was an Abyssinian?" Mark asked, bewildered.

"Yes, of course. An Aby. Why on earth would I say Siamese when I've been talking about an Abyssinian?" Orvenia commented in an exasperated tone.

Mark drove in silence. He knew Orvenia's quick temper and ugly mood swings. He'd just keep on driving until she spoke again, then he'd answer.

After a few minutes, Orvenia said, "I want to change my will."

"Sure, you can do that," Mark answered in a professional voice, but thought, 'here we go again.'

179

Orvenia had already changed her will many times, but maybe the thirteenth time's the charm. *More work*, he thought. *I bill by the hour.*

"I haven't heard from my Brooklyn relatives in a very long time. We didn't part on good terms. Everyone has died now, leaving only a great niece. Her name is Katherine. She works in Manhattan. Very bright girl. Works with computers."

"You've never mentioned a great niece before," Mark said curiously.

"Her mother named her daughter after me. My middle name is Katherine. Of course, you know that," Orvenia said matter-of-factly, "You being my attorney and all."

Katherine tried to turn in bed but couldn't move. She said out loud, "But you didn't know me. Mark found out about me through my social media page."

"Okay, no problem. We'll change your will," he said.

Orvenia smiled. "I want her to inherit everything, including this dear Abyssinian kitten we're picking up today. It means a lot to me. Erie people haven't been kind. They've always thought I married dear William for his money. I want Katz to have it."

Katherine forced herself to wake up. She was dizzy. She wanted another drink of water, but the man was gone. She heard a gun blast, then more shots. *Oh, my God, I've got to get out of here.*

# Chapter Eleven

Barbie drank more water and worried about Stevie going to the house. What should she do if she heard gun shots? Run? Limp to the house and try and help him? He had to be involved in drug dealing again, or why else would he come to Leonard's house? She knew Leonard got busted for marijuana once or twice, but thought he was clean now. This alternative medicine route was right up his alley, because several years ago he worked at the Erie Drug Store as a pharmacist.

Barbie sighed. *Leonard's always been so sweet to me,* she thought. *He knew how sensitive I was about my weight, so he made me diet shakes. But why was he so rough with me the last time I saw him? He's never done that before. Where did Jimmy take Leonard after he stabbed him? And why did the idiot bring him back? To murder him? But the Hulk was firing shots, too, or was that after Katz ran out of the house? It's just too confusing.*

*What a family I was born into*, she reflected sadly. *Stevie's starting a new business, but dear old Dad still has him tied to his business. When Jimmy stole my car and left with Leonard, they were empty-handed. When they came back, Jimmy was carrying a bag full of something. Leonard got out and seemed to be okay. I guess the wound wasn't as bad as I thought.*

Barbie hadn't waited for the two to come into the house. She limped back to the closet, where she waited until they went to sleep, then she left the house by the back door. Behind the house were several old sheds. She had chosen the one with the most junk, more things to hide behind.

Now, as she sat in Stevie's truck back at Townsend's house, the loud report of a rifle shot broke the silence. Barbie screamed and put her head down. She knelt down on the floorboard. The driver's side door opened and she looked up, expecting to see Stevie. Instead, it was the man with the disfigured face. He grunted something and motioned her to get out of the truck.

"I'm not gettin' out of this freakin' truck," she yelled. "Get outta here!"

"Hey, Buddy," Stevie yelled from up the road. "It's Stevie Sanders. I came to git my stuff. We're fixin to leave."

The man slammed the door and walked back into the woods.

Barbie shouted out the open truck window, "You know that man? What the hell!"

Stevie put several items in his diamond plate steel toolbox and hopped in. "He's some old geezer Leonard takes care of. Harmless, if he knows ya, but meaner than a snake if he doesn't."

"Harmless, you say? He's the one who pulled Katz out of the wreck. Call him back. We need to find her."

A loud clap of thunder rang through the woods. A bolt of lightning lit up the night sky and struck one of the nearby trees. The acrid smell of ozone permeated the air. Stevie shouted out his window. "Hey, Buddy, come back. I need to talk to ya." He yelled several more times, but the man didn't return.

Hail started hitting the truck: At first, small pellets the size of peas, then bigger hailstones. Stevie cursed, "Damn, not on my new truck! Hey, Barbie, I don't like the looks of this. Could be a tornado. Come on, we're goin' to Leonard's house."

"But I can hardly walk," she protested. "What if one of those hailstones hits us in the head?"

Stevie got out of the driver's side, pulled out a hooded jacket, and hurriedly put it on. He rushed over to Barbie. Opening the door, he said, "I'll carry you. Step down on the running board and I'll take it from there." Barbie did what she was told. Stevie leaned in, picked her up, and threw her over his shoulder. He began walking to the house. "You weigh a ton," he complained.

"Oh, really? You should have lifted me last Tuesday. I've lost a million pounds since then."

"Okay, shut up. Gotta concentrate on not droppin' you."

Stevie stepped around the tail end of the wrecked Subaru and nearly lost his footing, when he tripped over a piece from the wreckage—the rearview mirror. "Damn, about dropped you there."

"Hurry up. The hail is getting bigger. I just got hit by one," Barbie whined.

"I'm tryin'. I can see the porch light. Just a few."

When they got to the front porch, Stevie set Barbie down. The door was ajar, so he opened the screen door, stepped in, and flipped the inside light switch. Barbie limped in behind him. The wind slammed against the southwest side of the house, making the original glass windows rattle precariously in their frames.

Stevie found a flashlight. "Look, the power's goin' out any second. We've got to git down to the cellar."

"I *am not* goin' down there," Barbie said adamantly, easing into a chair.

"Hail usually comes before a twister, so . . ."

A large branch fell against the house. He yanked his sister out of the chair and threw her over his shoulder again. Holding the flashlight in his teeth, he opened the cellar door and slowly descended the stairs. Barbie collapsed against him.

"Did you faint?" he asked, cautiously taking one step at a time.

"No, I'm holdin' my breath. It really stinks down here."

"Just old house smell." He set her down and shone his light around the room. In the corner were two wood crates, so he picked them up and moved them to the center of the room. "Sit on one of these until the storm breaks." He walked back up the steps and turned on the light; a naked incandescent bulb shone dimly.

"You didn't come back here to get some tools," Barbie said in an accusing tone. "What was in your hand when you came back?"

Something heavy crashed into the house and the lights went out. Barbie screamed.

# Chapter Twelve

Katherine woke and tried to sit up on the bed. The pain in her ribs was too intense, so she lay back down. *What's that sound? Digging?* Someone was digging frantically in the closet—excavating. The sound seemed to go on forever. Scratch! Scratch! She heard Siamese mutterings nearby.

"I think it's covered," she said in the direction of the litterbox.

A brilliant flash of lightning lit up the room. A heavy wind gust slammed into the log cabin. The metal roof made a warping sound. Katherine could hear the front door opening and banging shut. "Oh, no. The door's open. My cats," she said aloud.

Abra soared off the moose head and landed next to her. "Raw," she cried sweetly in Katherine's ear.

"Where's Scout?" Katherine asked.

A loud clap of thunder spooked the cat and she shot off the bed, joining Scout in the closet.

"Scout," Katherine called in a weak voice. Scout was busy. She was making tiny "waugh" sounds as she dug on the carpet.

"What are you doing?" Katherine asked, now fully awake. "Get out of there."

Abra padded over to Scout and the two of them tugged at the carpet, pulling it away from the floor.

Katherine struggled to sit on the edge of the bed. She reached behind the small of her back and felt for the Glock. The waistband holster was there, but the gun was missing. "Dammit," she said, frustrated. She remembered the last time she had it was before the accident. *It must have fallen out the holster when I wrecked the Subaru*, she thought.

Another flash of lightning revealed a bottle of water sitting on the dresser. "I need water," she said to the cats.

"If it kills me, I'm getting off this bed and grab it." No sooner than she had one leg over, the man from the woods barged in. There was urgency in his step. The Siamese slinked to the back of the closet—safely out of view.

Katherine was no longer afraid of his disfigurement. She was more worried about the rifle he carried than the scars that lined his face. "Who are you?" she asked in a calm voice.

A large crow flew into the room and sat on the man's shoulder. "Caw," it said.

"My name is Katherine Kendall. My friends call me Katz."

The man placed his rifle on the foot of the bed. He removed a small chalkboard from his windbreaker's pocket. He also pulled out a piece of chalk and wrote: *Help you.*

"Thanks. I need to go to a hospital. Can you take me?"

The man wiped the board with his sleeve. *No phone*, he wrote. *Protect you. Man coming back.*

"The man who killed Mr. Townsend?"

He nodded.

"What happens now?"

*Move you*, he wrote.

"Where?" she asked, wincing at her pain.

*Give you something for pain.* The man removed a small ampoule and syringe from his shirt pocket.

"You're not giving that to me," Katherine objected. "I just need some Tylenol. Hand me my purse." Then she remembered her purse was in the Subaru.

The storm had grown in intensity. Hail began to hit the cabin, making loud crashing noises on the metal roof.

"We've got to go to an interior room," she shouted over the wind.

"Caw," the crow cried in alarm.

The man forcibly turned Katherine on her side and injected the needle into her hip.

Katherine screamed out in pain. "What did you just give me?"

The man gathered Katherine in his arms and took her to the closet where Scout and Abra had been digging. With one strong hand, he finished what the cats had started and ripped up the carpet panel to reveal a trap door, which he then lifted. He carried Katherine down some steps to a crawlspace, and carefully placed her on a blanket. Scout and Abra bolted down the steps and collapsed against Katherine's side.

The man walked to the corner of the crawlspace, pulled a lantern flashlight out of a plastic tub, and placed it next to Katherine. In the dim light, Katherine thought she saw him attempt a smile, but the scars prevented him from smiling.

"Caw! Caw!" the crow cried loudly from the top of the steps. The bird flew down and landed nearby. The man grumbled something to the crow, which the bird didn't seem to like. The crow started swaying rhythmically, flapping its wings. Scout hissed.

Exiting the crawlspace, the man tossed down a folded knife. It safely landed by Katherine's left side. He positioned the trap door back in place and left. Katherine could hear his footsteps overhead, as he walked toward the front of the cabin.

As Katherine drifted off into a morphine-induced sleep, she heard a man's voice shouting, "Hey, I just wanna talk to ya." The man yelled something else, but she couldn't understand his words. Then she heard two loud rifle shots.

# Chapter Thirteen

Jake paced the floor of the Atlanta airport. Staring at the departure board, he muttered, "This can't be good," under his breath. "All flights to Indianapolis cancelled." Heading over to a bar kiosk, he looked up at the wide-screen TV to monitor the local news. A middle-aged bartender came over and said, "What will it be?"

Jake found a bar stool and sat down. "A shot of bourbon. Hey, would you please turn the TV to the weather channel?"

"Sure," the bartender said, clicking the remote.

The meteorologist was discussing a supercell thunderstorm in the Midwest; several tornado sightings were reported in east central Illinois. The map on the screen didn't show a pretty picture. It looked like the entire state of Indiana had been painted red. She said, "Tornado warnings have been issued by the National Weather Service for these counties in Indiana, so if you're in this area, move to. . ." Jake was alarmed to see that a scrolling bar along the bottom of the screen included Erie County.

Jake removed his cell from his suit jacket and called Elsa. She answered the phone with panic in her voice. He could hear the Erie tornado sirens blaring in the background.

Elsa said breathlessly, "I can't talk. I'm herding cats to the basement."

Jake said, "I won't keep you."

"I've got most of the cats down there, but I can't find Lilac."

"Look underneath the wingback chair in the living room. Reach up inside the torn lining. Hurry! I'll call you later."

Jake put his cell on the bar. The bartender slid a shot glass over and Jake downed the golden liquid.

"Top you off?" the bartender asked.

Jake didn't answer right away. He thought back to when his wife, Victoria, had died. He was so lost, and had missed her so much. He couldn't deal with that pain, so he frequented taverns where he'd say *yes* to the bartender 'topping it off' many, many times.

But his life had turned around when he met Katz. He loved her. He shuddered to think about how empty his world would be without her.

The bartender interrupted the reverie. "Sir, another drink?"

"Oh, I'm sorry," Jake apologized, snapping out of it. "No thanks, but could you bring me a Coke?"

Jake picked up his cell and tapped his Dad's cell number. Johnny answered it right away.

"Howdy, son. Your mom and I are in the basement. Erie tornado sirens are blaring."

"Just saw the red blob on the weather map."

"The wind really kicked up in a hurry. Before we came down here, I saw Cokey's new grill fly by like a scene from *Wizard of Oz*. He won't be happy about that."

Jake proceeded to tell his father about being stuck in Atlanta, and his concerns about Katherine. Johnny said, "If you want me to, I'll drive to Peace Lake tomorrow and see if she's okay."

"Thanks, but I'm coming home tonight. As soon as I get to Indy, I'm driving to the cabin to check on her myself."

"Keep us posted."

"Sure thing, Dad. Text me when the storm's over, so I know you're okay?"

"Roger that."

Jake punched in Chief London's number, but the call went straight to voice mail. He sent a text instead: "Flight cancelled. Booked next flight to Indy, weather permitting. Should be there @ midnight. Find out anything about Katz?"

Jake didn't receive an answer until forty-five minutes later. While leaving the airport food court where he'd grabbed a bite to eat, the chief called. Jake read the name on his cell's screen and quickly answered. He moved to an area less-populated by weary travelers.

"Hey, Jake, are you still grounded?"

"No, flights are moving into Indy again. I'm taking the ten o'clock. Fortunately, it's a nonstop. Got any news for me?"

"Sheriff Johnson sent one of his deputies out to Townsend's. A powerful storm with heavy winds went through the area. It did extensive damage—trees down everywhere. He said it was a big mess."

"What about Katz?" Jake asked, wondering when the chief would get to the point of his call.

"There's a big oak tree blocking the road to Townsend's. His deputy couldn't get her cruiser more than a few feet off the highway. The power company is working to restore electricity, but rural customers will not be their highest priority. Since the tree is on private property, it will be up to Townsend to hire someone to cut it up and haul it away."

"Thanks, Chief. Are we still on to go to the cabin first thing tomorrow?"

"Sure. I'll pick you up. Where are you going to be stayin'?"

"At my parents' house. Can we leave at first light?" Jake asked.

"Yes, sounds like a plan. I'll call before I come over."

"Okay, thanks."

"Got another call. See ya tomorrow."

Jake thought, *I pray she's okay.* Katherine's well-being was always on his radar screen. His imagination was going wild with terrible things that could happen to her. He worried that the cabin didn't have a basement. Chances are it didn't. Would she know where to go during the storm? Did a tree fall on the house? Was there flooding? Were the cats okay? And, the most troubling question—was she in worse danger from Townsend than the storm? He rationalized, *She's got her Glock.*

# Chapter Fourteen

Stevie slowly climbed the cellar steps, not knowing what would greet him on the other side. "I hope there ain't a tree blockin' our way out."

Barbie demanded, "Hurry up and just open the door."

Stevie opened the door to find the living room windows shattered; shards of glass were everywhere. A large tree limb had crashed through the roof. Broken branches and leaves littered the room.

"Can we get out? I'm getting claustrophobic."

"Yeah, but I think we should wait until it's light outside to go back to my truck. I'm thinkin' there's a lot of storm damage. How about I go upstairs and find some sheets, blankets and stuff, and we sleep down here?"

"Not likin' that idea. It stinks worse down here."

Stevie didn't answer, but stepped up to the main floor and headed to the closest bedroom. Later, he returned with one pillow and two blankets. "This is all I could find. It's a mess up there. I'm wonderin' if the roof isn't goin' to cave in the front of the house."

"Are you sure we're safe down here?" Barbie asked. Her eyes had grown to the size of saucers.

Stevie spread the blankets on the floor and then the pillow.

"Who gets the pillow?" she asked.

Stevie teased. "I think we should flip a coin."

"No way. I get it. You're not the one living off of diet shakes the last three days. Leonard's refrigerator was practically empty."

"Just take it," Stevie smirked as he threw the pillow at her.

She caught it, then kneeled down and lay on the blanket. She winced. "My ankle is killing me. Do you think I broke it?"

"You wouldn't be hobblin' around if you did— probably a sprain."

"Stevie, there's something I really need to know. What did you really put in your truck? Was it drugs?"

"My tools," he said defensively. "I just bought that reciprocating saw—two hundred forty bucks."

"I saw you carrying two things."

"My ratchet-threader set was over six hundred dollars. Anything else you want to know about my business?"

"What was it doin' here?"

"There was a problem with the electrical at the cabin down the road—"

Barbie interrupted. "What cabin?"

"Leonard's vacation cabin. He rents it in the summer. I had to get the work done because the person was coming on Thursday. You're such buddies with Leonard. Looks like he would have told ya."

"Hells bells!" Barbie exclaimed. "That was Katz on Thursday. Why didn't I see her when she arrived?"

"As soon as it gets light, I'll head over there and check it out. Maybe the old geezer took her there."

Barbie changed the subject. "If I'd known Leonard was on Dad's payroll, I wouldn't have ever come out here."

"Payroll?" Stevie asked sheepishly.

"Yeah, Leonard's a drug dealer."

"Shhh," Stevie whispered, putting up his hand. "Did you hear that?"

They heard the back door slam and heavy footsteps above them. Stevie put the flashlight in his teeth, grabbed his gun, and aimed at the door. Barbie got up and crept to the corner. The door above creaked open, and a man stepped down several stairs. He held a handgun.

"So, Cuz," he said. "Would be nice if you took your gun off of me."

"Stay where you are, Jimmy," Stevie ordered.

"I woke up thinkin' that you'd come out here and get the dope."

"What dope?" Stevie asked. "I haven't seen any dope."

Jimmy observed Barbie for the first time, "What are you doin' here, Cuz?"

"I ain't your 'Cuz,' so stop sayin' it," Barbie answered. "Is somebody else with you?"

"No, does it look like it, stupid?"

Barbie shot Jimmy a dirty look, then thought fast on her feet. "I saw this big man with scars on his face take the drugs and head into the woods," she bluffed, hoping the not-so-bright Jimmy would leave and look for the Hulk, who had a rifle and seemed to know how to use it.

"You better not be lyin' to me, or I'm comin' back for you." Jimmy sprinted up the steps with Stevie following.

"Are you threatening us?" Stevie accused.

Jimmy didn't answer, and headed to the back of the house.

Stevie returned to the cellar. "Come on, sis. We've got to go someplace else and hide until morning. I don't trust Jimmy. He's liable to come back and shoot us."

"There's a shed behind the house. I know it well."

# Chapter Fifteen

"Get up, already," Katherine's mom scolded. "It's seven-thirty, and you'll be late for school."

"Mom, I'm sick. I don't feel good."

"Not one of your more creative excuses, but I've got to be at work at nine, and I thought we'd ride the subway together."

"Yes, Mom, but there isn't a subway in Erie."

"Of course not, silly goose. What are you babbling about? Get up," her mom said adamantly. Then in a serious tone, "If you're going to survive this, you must get up!"

"Okay," Katherine startled. Her brisk movement scared Scout and Abra, who were snuggled against her. Scout flinched.

"I'm sorry, my treasures. I had a bad dream—a sad dream. I miss my mom." A tear slid down from Katherine's eye.

Scout got up and did a full stretch; Abra snuggled up more.

"Oh, great," she said sarcastically. "We're still in the crawlspace." Carefully sitting up, she cried, "Ouch! Ouch!"

The lantern next to her was still on. Looking around, she could see that the crawlspace was a small area with a dirt floor. It had an earthy smell to it, and some other smell she couldn't quite identify.

It was daylight and she noticed that one end of the crawlspace was open to the outside. A crisscrossed wood lattice covered the opening, and tiny beams of light filtered through. She didn't know what the function of the lattice was, because clearly an animal or bird could get in and out without much effort.

"Where's the crow?" she asked the Siamese.

Abra blinked a kiss, got up and walked to the corner.

"I hope he's flown off to join his owner."

Scout's pink tongue was partially sticking out; she had a mischievous glint in her blue eyes. She trotted over to Katherine's right side and patted her paw on a bottle of water, an energy bar, and a very dead catfish.

"Yuck, that's the smell," Katherine said, scooching back. She opened the bottle and drank most of it, then ate the energy bar. The Siamese looked at her curiously. Scout cried, "Waugh," which sounded like "Are you going to eat the fish or not?"

"Thank you, Scout, but I'll let you share it with your sister."

Scout licked her lips.

"Oh, no, you didn't just do that. Do me a favor, drag it off somewhere else to eat it. I never was a fan of sushi."

Abra began digging frantically in the corner.

Katherine said, "You better join Scout. She's got breakfast."

Abra continued digging. With great effort, she jerked something out of the soil, and with several hard whacks, batted it over. Katherine followed the action with great interest and was startled to see what it was—her missing Glock.

"Stop, Abra! Let me have it." Katherine slowly got to her hands and knees. Lifting the gun, she could see the magazine was missing, and assumed there probably wasn't a bullet in the chamber either. She racked the slide and was surprised to eject a bullet.

Picking up the bullet, she said, "Okay, cats, this is a stroke of good luck."

Abra cried "raw" and returned to the hole. She began digging again. She brought up an object and tried to hold it in her jaws, but it was too heavy. Undaunted, she gave the Glock's magazine several hockey-worthy hits and it skidded and spun over to Katherine.

"Amazing," Katherine said, taking it. "Come here for some power pets." Abra came over and rubbed her face on Katherine's leg. Katherine petted Abra on the head and praised, "Good girl. I'm not going to ask you why my gun was over there or how you just found it, but . . ."

Suddenly, a roar of chain saws sounded from the distance. Katherine remembered the great number of tall trees bordering either side of the lane. She imagined that a lot of them must have fallen in the storm. "Okay, my furry little friends, I'm going to force myself up the steps and get us out of here." She picked up the Glock's magazine, which was fully loaded. She used the bottom of her tank top to clean the outside and the top of the clip, where the last bullet was exposed. She tried to get as much dirt off as possible. She did the same for the handgun, then slid the magazine into the Glock. She pushed the gun into its holster in the back of her jeans and inched toward the stairs.

Heavy footsteps sounded overhead. It sounded like two people were chasing each other. There was a scuffle, and then a loud thud against the floor. Someone yelled, "Drop your weapon."

Katherine said determinedly, "We're getting out of here—now!"

Scout bounded over to the wood lattice and pushed it. It swung open.

Katherine gasped in wonder, "It's a gate." Crawling outside, she saw the pond for the first time in the early morning daylight. The water was a brilliant green, and had a foggy haze over it. It had a surreal quality. Maybe it was the effects of the drug the man had given her, but she turned her gaze to the pond. She saw someone walking out of it—a man dressed in an army uniform.

She squeezed her eyes shut, then opened them. The apparition was gone. *I've just seen the ghost of Peace Lake. But this isn't the lake,* she thought, *it's a pond.* Slowly inching outside, Katherine called to the cats, "Please stay with me. Don't run off. If you do, I'll never find you. I'm going to try and get help."

Moving at a snail's pace—with the cats staying surprisingly close to her —Katherine crawled to the corner of the house and was about to go farther when she heard an angry voice in the crawlspace. "I know you're down here. Where's the freakin' Oxy?"

The fur on the back of Scout and Abra rose and their tails bushed out. Scout growled and Abra hissed. A large striped skunk waddled through the gate into the crawlspace.

The man shouted more. "Hey, back off. Get the hell out of here. You just sprayed me, you little bastard."

The skunk ran out unharmed, paused just outside the lattice, and shot a glance at Katherine and the cats, seeming to say, "My work here is done." Flicking his tail, he scampered off in the opposite direction. Jimmy launched out of the crawlspace, threw his gun on the ground, and dashed toward the pond, taking off his clothes as he ran. Katherine and the cats didn't have time to react and were surprised when they saw Chief London, with his service revolver poised to shoot, jogging after Jimmy.

"Stop right there," the Chief ordered. He aimed his revolver at Jimmy, who put his hands up, then leaped into the water.

"Get out of there," the Chief thundered. Jimmy reluctantly got out and stood shivering on the bank. Chief London cuffed him, complaining the entire time. "I'm gonna need a new cruiser after this."

A deputy bolted out of the crawlspace and rushed down to help the chief.

Katherine sat down in the grass, holding onto both Siamese; Scout was squirming to be set free.

"Quit it!" Katherine admonished.

"Katz," Jake called, running up beside her. He kneeled down and started to embrace her, but stopped when he saw the bruises on her face. He kissed her on the top of her head, instead. "Are you in pain?"

"Only when I breathe—my chest and ribs hurt like hell. How did you know to look for me here?"

"Back at Townsend's house, the chief and I talked to Stevie and Barbie Sanders. They said Jimmy Sanders was armed, and they thought he was heading for the cabin. We got back in the cruiser and the chief radioed for some backup. Just as we pulled in the drive, we saw Jimmy on the front porch. A deputy pulled up quickly behind us. He followed Jimmy into the cabin while the chief walked to the front."

"Why's Barbie *here*?"

"Barbie has been here since she left the mansion last Tuesday. She said she's been hiding from drug dealers."

Abra cried an impatient, "Raw."

"It will be just a minute, sweet girl," Katherine said, and then thought, *Barbie must have been the crazy lady I saw dart out from behind a tree. She caused my accident.* "Jake," she asked, "Why's Stevie here?"

"Yesterday Stevie drove here to pick up some tools he'd left behind. He was doing electrical work for Townsend last Monday and forgot them."

Katherine thought suspiciously, *Likely story.* "How's Barbie?"

"She's fine, except she sprained her ankle. Right now she's sitting in one of the deputies' cars giving a statement, then Stevie is driving her to urgent care in Erie."

The emergency crew with the chain saws was getting closer. The loud noises frightened the Siamese, who wriggled to get free. It was getting difficult for Katherine to continue holding the hyperactive cats.

Jake said, getting up, "I'll be right back." He returned shortly with their cat carrier. "I found this on the cabin porch. I'm surprised the wind didn't blow it away." Jake opened the metal gate and placed Scout and Abra inside. He petted them before he shut the door. "You'll be home soon," he whispered in a soothing voice.

"Jake, can we get out of here? My cabin adventure would make a great script for a B movie, but I don't want to draw it out any more than I have to. I need to go to the hospital." She heard the sound of an ambulance off to the west, roaring down the main highway.

"Yes, Sweet Pea," Jake smiled. "I'm so thankful you weren't seriously injured in the accident."

"How's the ambulance going to get back here? My SUV's probably in the way."

"When the chief and I arrived, there were three vehicles blocking the lane. Sheriff Johnson and his deputies were already on the scene, so the sheriff called in for a couple of tow trucks. Once they towed the blue pickup, Stevie was able to back out and park on the shoulder of the main drag. Now there's a bunch of guys cutting branches and removing debris. They've cleaned up half of the lane, so there's enough room for an ambulance to get through."

"The guy who drives the blue pickup tried to force me off the road."

Jake nodded in the direction of Jimmy Sanders. "The truck belongs to him. He's Stevie's cousin."

Katherine shook her head. "My head's swimming. None of this makes any sense to me."

"I'm sorry, Katz. The ambulance will be here any minute. The Sheriff said you were forced off the road by Jimmy. There's blue paint marks on the driver's side of your SUV. Once we found you weren't pinned in Sue-Bee . . ." Jake's voice broke, then he collected himself. "Katz, your SUV was upside-down in a drainage ditch. The tow driver had to pull it out with a winch before he could load it on a flatbed wrecker. It's a miracle you survived the crash."

She thought, *I survived the crash because of the man in the woods. I'm worried about him. After he carried me to the crawlspace and left, I heard shots being fired. Did Jimmy kill him?* "Jake, will you ride in the ambulance with me?"

"Yes, Sweet Pea."

"What about my cats? How are they going to get home?"

"My Dad's on his way. I texted him when we got here. He'll take them home."

"I never met Mr. Townsend," Katherine began shakily. "When I arrived here, there was an envelope with the cabin key in it tucked inside his front screen door. In hindsight, I should have just driven back home."

"And I wish you would have, too," Jake said seriously. "Elsa said Scout and Abra were very upset when you left, and that's why you ended up taking them. We need to listen to them. They're smarter than we are."

"Ma-waugh," Scout agreed inside the carrier.

"Did they find a body?"

"What?" Jake asked, surprised.

"The cats and I stayed one night and then decided to leave. It's a long story, and my ribs hurt too much to go into detail, but we left around one p.m. There was a beat-up blue pickup parked in front of Mr. Townsend's house. I thought it was his truck. I walked up to the house to return the key, but he didn't answer the door. It was open, so I walked in, calling for him. That's when I heard the gunshot in the backyard. So I ran to the kitchen window and saw that guy over there—Jimmy Sanders—holding a gun and standing over a man, who was lying face-down. I assumed it was the cabin owner."

"What are you talking about? You witnessed a shooting?"

"Unfortunately, the answer is yes."

"Right now they're arresting Jimmy for criminal recklessness with a vehicle and fleeing an officer."

"Oh, it's a lot more than that."

Sheriff Johnson and another deputy arrived and walked down to the shore. They took the prisoner from Chief London and headed up the side yard next to the cabin.

"Chief London," Jake called.

Chief London came over. "Katz, you look pretty banged up. There's an ambulance on its way."

"I'm not doing any fashion shows today," Katherine answered wearily.

"We meet again under unusual circumstances. Katz, sometimes I think you need a rabbit's foot the size of an elephant," the chief remarked.

"It seems since I've moved to Erie, I've become a murder magnet."

"What's up? Spit it out," the chief said, tugging his beard.

Katherine relayed to the chief what she had just told Jake.

"You're absolutely sure it was Jimmy Sanders?" he asked.

"One-hundred-percent sure," Katherine said.

"Did you fire on Jimmy when he tried to run you off the road?"

Katherine shook her head.

"I see you have your weapon. Can I see it?"

"Of course," Katherine said, as she pulled the Glock out of its holster. She started to hand the gun to the chief.

"Wait just a second." He pulled a pen out of his shirt pocket and stuck it in his mouth. Then he extracted an evidence bag, inserted the pen in the gun barrel, and placed the Glock in the bag. "When was the last time you cleaned your gun?"

"I'm sorry to say I lost it after my accident. It wasn't on me when I woke up. My cat just dug it up in the crawlspace."

"Pull the other one, it's got bells on it," the chief said, joking. "Seriously, your cat?"

"I know it sounds crazy."

"You can tell me that story another day," he said, then went back into official police chief mode. "Did you shoot the back windshield out of Jimmy's truck?"

"No, I was too busy trying to stay on the road."

The chief held up the evidence bag. "The Sheriff will want to do a ballistic test on your weapon, especially since you said you lost it for a while. You'll get it back."

"Not a problem. I don't think I'll be needing it anyway. I'm in good hands," Katherine said, as she smiled at Jake.

"Okay, I've got to talk to the Sheriff. I'll suggest he get your statement at the hospital. I'll meet you two there."

The chief hurried off in the direction of the sheriff.

A large crow flew overhead and landed nearby. He moved from side-to-side, hopped up and down, and "cawed" loudly. He eyed the cats in the carrier, then flapped his wings and soared to the woods behind the cabin.

Jake eyes grew big. "Wow, that's the biggest crow I've ever seen!"

Katherine gave a quick glance toward the woods. She thought she saw her rescuer standing at the edge, but in an instant he was gone. Scout and Abra were looking in that direction, as well.

"Caw," Abra cried. "Raw."

The ambulance arrived and two paramedics climbed out. One was carrying a large EMT bag, while the other stayed behind, removing a gurney from the back of the bus. The first paramedic rushed over to Katherine. "What's your name?"

"Katherine."

"I saw your wreck back there. Can you tell me where it hurts?"

"My chest and ribs."

He pulled out his blood pressure cuff and placed it around Katherine's arm. Listening carefully through a stethoscope, he said, "Blood pressure is a little high." Feeling her pulse, "Pulse is pounding like a racehorse's. Are you bleeding anywhere?"

"No, I don't think so."

To Jake, he asked, "Are you the husband?"

"No, but I want to be."

Katherine grinned.

"Miss, are you able to stand up?"

"Yes, I think I can, if someone helps me. . ." She tried to get up, but then sat back down. A tidal wave of pain rippled through her ribs. "A stretcher would do me just fine."

# Chapter Sixteen

Stevie waited impatiently outside the back entrance of his father's bar—the Dew Drop Inn. Sam Sanders pulled up in his new Toyota Tundra pickup. Stevie threw his cigarette on the gravel and extinguished it with his foot. He had an angry expression on his face.

Sam got out of his truck and walked over. "Nasty habit, son."

"Same to you, Dad," Stevie said with an arrogant tone.

"What's eatin' you?"

"Was it really smart to abandon Barbie's car in Shermanville? Wasn't that a little bit too close to the storage unit? You could have led the cops right to our back door."

Sam glared for a moment, then said, "The original plan was for Leonard to drive up and get the Oxy, like he always does. But his car was being worked on, so I asked

Jimmy to drive. I didn't count on Jimmy stabbing Leonard. I picked them up at a closed rest stop and took them to a buddy of mine, who patched the old guy up. After that, we went to the storage unit so we could pick up the stuff. By the time we got back to Barbie's car, the cops were all over it like ticks on a deer."

"Why involve Leonard in the first place? You had the Oxy. Why didn't you take care of it in Chicago?"

"Are you stupid? Leonard packs it for shipping," Sam said angrily.

"Don't ever call me stupid," Stevie threatened. "I'm done, Dad. This was the last time I help you out with your business."

"Why is that?"

"Because I'm goin' legit—no more drug pickups, no more of your dirty work."

"So where is it?" his father asked without empathy.

Stevie lifted a black grocery bag and shoved it at his dad. "Tell me, was it worth it for a man we've known forever to be murdered . . . over *this*?"

"Gettin' sentimental on me, son? You had a job to do and you did it," Sam said, then paused. "Oh, I get it. Does this change of vocation to the electrical business have anything with Katz Kendall?"

Stevie scowled. "She's the witness—the only witness, since Jimmy's dead."

Sam put his hands up. "I had nothing to do with that fool hangin' himself at the county jail. How do you think I felt, tellin' his poor mama he was dead?"

Stevie looked at his father with disgust. "Seems rather convenient to me, Jimmy dyin'. Now he won't be testifyin'. If he would have lived, he would have ratted us out. I've done time once. I ain't goin' back there again!"

"Son, you worry too much. There's nothing that can link us to the old man's death. Nothing," Sam emphasized.

"The Kendall woman saw Jimmy shoot Townsend. According to my inside source, the cops found drugs at Leonard's, but not the Oxy. Case closed."

Stevie turned and started for his truck.

Sam grabbed his arm. "Don't go off half-cocked."

"Let go of me," Stevie demanded, shoving away his father's arm. "*Never, ever*," he enunciated each word, "go near Katz. If she ever dies mysteriously, I'm comin' for you. Got that? Now do me a big-time favor—never call me again. I'm done! Done!" Stevie climbed into his pickup, started the engine, and drove out, almost hitting Sam's new truck.

Sam shrugged nonchalantly, picked up the bag of Oxy, and put it in his truck. He locked the doors, then went inside and sat at the bar. "Hey, Eddie, line up a couple of shots of tequila. Oh, hell, drinks all around. I'm in a celebrating kind of mood," he laughed.

# Chapter Seventeen

*A MONTH LATER—MID-AUGUST*

Katherine stood behind the front door of the pink mansion, waiting for Barbie to show up. Iris was rubbing against her leg and purring loudly.

"It's okay, Miss Siam. She'll be here in a minute."

Barbie pulled in front and parked her loaner car—a red Ford Focus. Her Mustang was still impounded by the Shermanville police until the Leonard Townsend investigation was finished. She got out of the vehicle and walked up the front steps in her soft walking cast.

Katherine opened the door, "Hi, Barbie. Come in."

"Oh, ha! Ha! What do you think of my new kicks? Ain't I a fashion plate?"

Dewey and Crowie ran out to greet her. Barbie sat down on an Eastlake chair and picked up the kittens, kissing them repeatedly on their heads. "Mommy has missed you so much. You're coming home today," and to Katherine, "Thanks so much for taking care of them. I love their new collars."

"Oh, Jake bought them because the other ones were too small. The kittens are growing in leaps and bounds."

Iris stood in the corner, looking sad that Barbie hadn't noticed her. She ran out of the room and hid behind the Eastlake coat tree.

Katherine followed the cat with her eyes, then said, "It's been my pleasure, but your cousin, Elsa, did the major cat wrangling."

"I'll have to thank her. How are you feeling?"

"Although it's been a month since my cabin adventure from hell, my doctor said it could take several more weeks for my ribs to heal."

"Heal? I didn't think your ribs were broken."

Katherine sat down, carefully. "I didn't mean heal, I meant for my ribs to stop hurting. The treatment for bruised ribs is the same as if I *had* broken them. It seems my injury was to the muscles surrounding the ribs."

"Did you get your new car?"

"Yes, Sue-bee Two—as Jake calls her—is parked in the back. I got a sleek black one this time—like the color of Stevie's truck."

"Oh, Stevie," Barbie dismissed. "I haven't talked to him since the whole Leonard mess."

"Why's that?"

"Because," she answered evasively. "Let's just leave it at that. Did you hear they found Leonard's body last week?" she asked, changing the subject.

"Detective Martin called me. Someone had buried Leonard in an old cemetery plot on his property. They suspect Jimmy Sanders did it, but at the burial site, they didn't find his prints, or any of the tools used to bury the body."

"I'm surprised. Jimmy's lights were on, but nobody was home. Katz, I couldn't imagine Jimmy doin' all that physical labor to bury poor Leonard. Do you think that horrible Hulk man in the woods did it?"

"Hulk man? Is that what you call him? That so-called horrible man saved my life," Katherine countered. "I can't imagine how he'd have time to bury a man when he was taking care of me."

"Just thinkin' out loud."

"Detective Martin said the gun used to kill Leonard belonged to Jimmy. There was gunshot residue on Jimmy's hands, which confirms he shot Leonard. The investigators believe the reasons why—the motive —is your cousin, Jimmy, killed Leonard Townsend over illegal drugs."

"Stevie's cousin," Barbie corrected. "Actually, no blood relation to either one of us. My Dad's brother, Uncle Harlon, remarried a woman who had two sons. He adopted both of them. One of them was Jimmy. In high school,

Jimmy and Stevie were pretty tight and called each other cousin, then later went their separate ways."

"There is one thing that doesn't make any sense to me. Why would Leonard and Jimmy take your car, then abandon it?" Katherine asked.

Barbie shrugged. "Beats me. I think Jimmy stole it because he didn't think his piece of junk would make the trip."

"Why Shermanville? What's there?" Katherine asked curiously.

"I don't know. I've never been there." Barbie set the kittens down. Dewey cried a loud "Mao," and the two kittens scampered upstairs. She sighed, "I just want my car back. I've talked to my insurance agent to see if they'll pay to replace the back seat. The thought of blood stains in my new car is disgusting."

"Detective Martin said the forensics team did a bloodstain pattern analysis. She said the blood matched Leonard's."

"Do these people not read statements? I could have told them it was Leonard's blood," Barbie said sarcastically. "I saw the poor man get stabbed."

"I need to ask you something, and I don't want you to get mad."

"Fire away."

"If Jimmy left his pickup at Leonard's, why didn't you use that vehicle to escape?"

Barbie became defensive. "I didn't have the keys. I may be jack-of-all-trades, but I don't know how to hot-wire a car!"

"Previously you said when Jimmy and Leonard returned, they were in the blue pickup. How is that possible when Jimmy stole your car and left the truck?"

"I didn't say that. When they returned, I could hear them talking in the yard. Then I hid in the closet."

"But Barbie, why would you have to hide from Jimmy Sanders?"

"Oh, ha! Ha!" Barbie laughed uncomfortably. "You need to give up your computer training classes and go into law enforcement. What's with the twenty questions?"

"It was a traumatic event for me. I just want to understand."

"Jimmy has a terrible temper, and it's even worse when he's had a few beers. When he first came to Leonard's, he was drunk. I could hear him slurring his words. Leonard was protecting me by telling me to hide. He demanded my car keys because he wanted to get away. I think he was goin' into town to get help, and then come back."

"But wouldn't Jimmy know that was your new car parked outside, and that you had to be inside the house? All he'd have to do was look for your registration in the glove compartment."

"I don't keep my registration there. I keep it in my purse. I just bought my car. How would Jimmy know it was mine? Besides Katz, I've said all this stuff in my statement. Not to be a jerk about it, but do you want a copy of it?"

Katherine didn't answer. "Where's your purse now? Didn't you say Leonard took it?"

"The Shermanville police have it and said that when I pick up my car, they'd return it then, or I could drive up there and get it sooner. I'll just wait, because I've had time to cancel my credit cards and get a new driver's license."

"That being the case, Jimmy could have looked in your bag at your wallet and known the car was yours. Is that why you were so afraid and hid? You were afraid Jimmy would come looking for you? Has he hurt you before?"

"Yes, Officer Kendall," Barbie said irritably.

"I'm sorry," Katherine apologized. "I hate to ask these questions, but they've really been bugging me. Okay, let's get back to the day I had my accident. Someone else must have dropped Jimmy and Leonard off and they walked to the house."

"Stevie said that man in the woods worked for Leonard. Maybe he brought them back. I really don't know."

"That could explain why he was in the vicinity when I crashed."

Barbie's face lit up. "That has to be it. The Hulk has some kind of connection, some kind of role in all of this. Are you going to tell the Sheriff?"

"I'm not convinced the man in the woods had anything to do with what happened. I think he's a recluse with a medical condition. He couldn't speak, but he was able to write on a chalkboard. Leonard was a kind soul to take care of him."

"If you do tell the Sheriff, he'll want to question him. How's he gonna find him? Katz, Leonard owns—I mean owned—hundreds of acres. It would take a lot of cops to search that area. It would be like findin' a needle in a haystack. Katz, I'm very good at keepin' secrets," Barbie said, shifting the conversation. "I haven't told anyone else, except for Stevie, about the Hulk, because I'm tired of people thinkin' I'm nuts. You gotta admit it. It's a crazy story."

Katherine agreed. "You think people would think you're nuts, how about me? I told the police Leonard's body was in the backyard. When they didn't find the body, they looked at me like I had three heads."

Barbie laughed, which relieved some of the tension.

Katherine smiled, then said, "Thank you, Barbie. I don't plan on telling anyone about what you've told me. I've told Jake my story, but I don't think he's fully convinced there was/is such a person. As soon as I can, I'm going back to the cabin and try to find him."

"You're going back there? Are you crazy? Why?" Barbie asked with disbelief.

"He's an unsolved mystery. I want to find out who he is. Does he have any family who could help him? I *want* to help him."

"If I were you, I'd wait until the cops clear the area. Or worst-case scenario, you'd go out there and get arrested for trespassing. Talk to Leonard's son, Roger. He inherited the place."

"Wow, Barbie, how do you know this stuff?"

"I went to the funeral a few days ago. I talked to his son, who was in my class in high school. He lives in Erie. I'm sure he'd rent the cabin to you. He'd probably sell it to you. He gave me the idea he didn't want anything to do with his dad's property."

"I'm not sure I'm staying at the cabin. Jake and I are driving out there for the day—soon, I hope."

"For a second there, I thought you were goin' to ask me to go. I'd rather die before I went back to that place," Barbie said, getting up. "Katz, tell me where the carrier is so I can take my babies home."

"Cokey's working in the basement. I'll text him and ask him to help you carry them out."

"No need. I'm getting around pretty good in my soft boot."

Katherine thought, *If that's the case, why did you wait so long to pick them up?* She bit her tongue and didn't say it.

"Their carrier is in the parlor. I'd get it for you, but I can't lift things yet."

Barbie went into the parlor and picked up the carrier. "Dewey! Crowie! Come to mommy," she said, setting it down.

The kittens bounded down the steps.

Katherine got up, "I want to say good-bye." She picked them up and kissed each one of them on the back of their necks. "I'll miss you, you little monkeys." Iris slinked in the room and yowled softly. "Iris will miss you, too."

Barbie reached down and put the kittens in the carrier.

"Oh, Barbie, before I forget. Dr. Sonny has the kittens on a special diet so they'll gain weight. He said they were too small for their age."

"Yeah, I guess I kinda suspected that. Leonard was making their food, too."

Katherine thought, *Why is this woman so gullible?* Katherine walked to a marble-top curio and grabbed a tub of prescription canned cat food. "Directions are on the can. He said you should take them in to be reweighed in two weeks."

"Thanks, Katz, for everything. I'll be in touch soon." Barbie put the tub on top of the carrier, reached down, and picked up the cage.

Katherine moved over to the door and opened it for her. "Take care now. I hope to see you soon. Next time you're in town, bring the kittens over for playtime," Katherine said, closing the door.

Katherine suddenly felt very sad. She had gotten very attached to the kittens, and now they were gone. She wondered if she'd ever see them again. She sensed that her friendship with Barbie was waning. Barbie seemed to know more than what she was telling. Katherine didn't trust her anymore.

Iris walked over with her head down and her tail between her legs. She threw herself against Katherine. "Yowl," she cried.

Katherine picked her up and held the seal-point against her chest. "I understand, sweetheart. I'll miss them, too. And I'm sorry Barbie was too busy to hold you."

Iris reached up and affectionately bit Katherine on the ear.

"Thanks, I appreciate the love bite, too."

# Chapter Eighteen

It was movie night at the mansion. Jake and Katherine sat on the faux-leather sofa in the living room. Jake had his foot up on the ottoman. It was Katherine's turn to pick the movie, but she decided to let Scout and Abra make the final selection. In a shallow cardboard box she placed three DVDs: *Birdman of Alcatraz, Salmon Fishing in the Yemen,* and *The Village.*

Scout looked in the box and then at Katherine; she hiked up her tail and left the room, muttering a barrage of Siamese. Abra tipped the box over and began a game of hockey with the three movies. Finally, she stood on top of *The Village.*

Katherine asked, "Is this your final answer?"

Abra cried, "Raw."

"Good girl," Jake praised. "Let's see which one you picked." He got up, grabbed the DVD, and then sat back down. "And the winner is M. Night Shyamalan's *The Village*."

"Have you seen it?" Katherine asked, giving Abra a curious look. The Siamese hopped onto the credenza and stood in a regal pose, next to the fifty-inch flat screen. She crossed her eyes, lifted her back leg, and began to clean her toes.

Jake said to Abra, "Catfish fishing in Erie County doesn't appeal to you?" He laughed, then asked Katherine, "What's *The Village* about?"

"It's about a tightly knit community living in secret, surrounded by woods."

"Should I hum a few bars of The *Twilight Zone*? It's strange Abra would pick a movie that's reminiscent of your experience at the cabin—only in your case, it was a man living in secret in the woods."

"Jake, can we skip the movie? There's something I need to talk to you about."

"Sure. What's up?" A wave of concern rushed over his face.

"Can you keep a secret?"

"Yes, what's this about?"

"Will you promise to keep what I tell you in the strictest of confidence?"

"You mistake me for a lawyer. But of course."

There was an uncomfortable silence between them.

"Okay, tell me, Katz," Jake prodded.

"I didn't pull myself out of the wreckage and crawl back to the cabin."

"Katz, we've been over this. There were bruises on the palms of your hands. Your knees were black-and-blue from crawling. The ER doctor said you probably suffered a concussion and were having difficulty remembering exactly what happened."

"I remember being pulled out of the wreck by a man. He took me to the cabin and took care of me. He gave me a drug to help my pain. During the storm, he carried me down to the crawlspace."

Jake grabbed her hand and held it. He began slowly, "Katz, you said that when you left the cabin, you placed the cat's carrier on the cargo area of the Subaru. Then you said after you saw the shooting, you ran to your vehicle and the cat carrier was gone. Yet when I arrived at the cabin, the carrier was on the front porch and the cats were with you. How do you explain that?"

"I can't. Maybe I did leave the cats at the cabin when I left, but I most certainly wouldn't have left them outside, in their crate. They would have been inside. I probably was going to drop off the key and go back for them. I must have hit my head on something when I crashed, which explains why my memory is so foggy. But I do remember the man pulling me out of the wreckage and how I hurt like hell. Is it possible he took the cats out of my vehicle when I went into Leonard's to return the key?"

Jake shook his head. "I don't think so, Katz."

"I remember the crawlspace. The lantern and the knife —"

Jake interrupted, "What knife?"

"The one he gave me. He threw it down to me in the crawlspace before he closed the trap door."

"Interesting," Jake said. "Do you think it's possible the knife is still there?"

"I wouldn't think so. It seems the police would have thoroughly searched the area. But it's worth a try to go back and see for ourselves."

"I'm game."

"If I find it, will you believe me then?" Katherine asked with a hopeful look.

Jake leaned over and kissed her on the cheek. "It's not that I doubt you, it's that I'm just trying to analyze the facts."

"Yes, Professor."

"On second thought, do you think it's wise to go back to the scene of one of your worst nightmares?"

"One thing I learned from my grief counseling: The best way of recovering from a traumatic event is to go back and face it head-on."

"When do you want to go?"

"Actually, I'd like to go tomorrow."

Scout joined Abra on the credenza, "Ma-waugh."

Katherine answered, "No, you two are *not* going this time."

Jake said, "It's going to be a nice day. Want to take the Jeep, or Sue-bee Two?"

"The Jeep's fine."

*     *     *

Katherine used an app on her phone to find Leonard
Townsend's son's phone number and tapped the number.
Roger answered, "Erie Hardware."

"I'm sorry. I must have rang the wrong number."

"Who ya lookin' for?"

"Roger Townsend."

"Well, that would be me. I had my house phone
forwarded here because I'm working late. How can I help
you?"

"My name is Katherine Kendall. I'm sorry about
your father."

"Your name rings a bell. Are you the woman who
rented the cabin and then had a terrible car crash by my
dad's house?"

"Yes, that's me. I hate to bother you, but I left a
vintage brooch at the cabin," she lied. "It's not worth

253

anything, but it has sentimental value. My mom gave it to me. I was wondering if I could drive out to the cabin and look for it?"

"I see no problem with that, but you'll have to come to the hardware store to get the key. I open tomorrow at nine."

"Thank you so much. I'll be there first thing."

"Okay, but before I hang up, be careful out there, especially when you go past my dad's house. I had it bulldozed, and there's lots of debris around," Roger said, hanging up.

Katherine started to say good-bye, but realized Roger had ended the call.

*    *    *

The next morning, Jake picked Katherine up and drove her to Erie Hardware to get the key. He sat in the Jeep while Katherine went inside. Roger was behind the front counter, and Katherine introduced herself.

Roger said, "You know, I asked my wife if she knew who you were, and she said you're that millionaire who lives in the pink mansion."

Katherine was uncomfortable with the millionaire reference, and wondered where the conversation was heading.

"I've got a little business proposition," he continued. "I'll sell you the cabin and the surrounding land as soon as the estate is in a position to sell."

Katherine startled. "I hadn't really considered it. Can I take it under advisement?"

"Sure. After I have a real estate appraisal done, I'll give you a call."

"Okay, thanks."

Roger handed her the key.

"What time are you closing, so I make sure I get the key back."

"Four o'clock."

"My ride's outside," Katherine said. "I better get going. Nice meeting you."

"Likewise," Roger said.

The bell over the door jingled lightly, and a customer came in.

*     *     *

"Look familiar?" Jake asked, as he turned the Jeep into the late Leonard Townsend's lane. The road was full of deep ruts, so Jake put the vehicle into four-wheel drive, and tried to avoid hitting them.

"Not really," Katherine said, looking out her window. "It was raining when I arrived."

"How far down is Townsend's?"

"Not far."

They came to a clearing in the woods where Leonard's house had been. Now ugly piles of lumber and roofing material were stacked in rough rows. The sheds in back had been bulldozed, too.

"Pull up here," Katherine said, looking at the site. "That's where the house was. It was a quaint Eastlake farmhouse. It had a lot of potential. Margie would have loved to get her hands on it."

Jake stopped. "The woods are beautiful, but this place is a mess. I wonder if Roger will rebuild on it."

"I got the impression he wanted to sell it as soon as Leonard's estate is closed."

Jake noted, "It's bound to be worth a lot of money."

"Okay, I've seen enough," she announced abruptly.

Jake pulled forward and continued while Katherine gave him directions. Finally, they came to the cabin. Jake parked and got out. Katherine did the same. The cicadas began whining their deafening song, then fell quiet. The sun shone brightly, not a cloud in the sky. The cabin and the pond looked like a scene on a postcard.

"It's really nice out here," Jake admired. "The cabin looks brand-new. I guess I lost the bet. I don't see an old car jacked up on blocks."

"Wait until you see the inside," she said, stepping up on the porch and opening the door. She showed Jake throughout the cabin, and then into the closet where the trap door was. "I'd lift this up," she said, "but my ribs are sore from the drive here. Can you do it?"

"Sure," Jake said, leaning down. He grabbed the handle and removed the trap door. "Katz, let me go down first so I can help you." Jake climbed down and held his hand out for Katherine.

Once on the dirt floor, she looked around. It was dimly lit. Jake went back upstairs to turn on the light, but it didn't work.

"The bulb's broken," Katherine noted. She got down on her hands and knees and began looking in the area where the blanket was. "There was a blanket here," she explained. "That's where the man put me down."

Jake took out a pocket flashlight and shone the light on the area.

In the vicinity of where the blanket was, Katherine began digging the loose dirt with her hands. She dug for several minutes, then said, frustrated, "I'm sorry I brought you out here. I can't find it."

Before Jake had time to answer, Katherine said excitedly, "Wait a minute! What's this?" She felt a cold object and lifted it up.

"Wow, you did find it. Let's go back upstairs and clean it up."

Heading to the kitchen, Katherine dampened a washrag and began cleaning the knife. It was heavily soiled. After she finished washing it, she dried it with a towel.

Jake reached over and took it, "Let me see. This is a serrated hunter's fold-back knife. Here's the manufacturer's mark," he said, pointing it out to Katherine. "And here's where a person usually had it engraved."

"You're kidding me. People engrave their knives? Do you see anything?" Katherine asked hopefully.

"I can't. Let's take it out into the sunlight where the light's better."

They both left the cabin and sat on the front step. "Yes, I see—"

"Is there a name?"

"No, just initials," Jake said eagerly. "E. H."

Katherine face dropped. "That doesn't mean anything. That could be anyone."

"Yeah, anyone with those initials."

"Okay, so we don't know who the knife belongs to, but we have the initials."

"Use the phone directory app on your cell to look up everyone in Peace Lake whose last name begins with an 'H,'" Jake suggested.

Katherine extracted her cell from her back pocket and tapped the app icon. "There's not that many Hs, and none of the first names starts with E. I mean, what kind of name begins with E?" she asked, exasperated.

"Elmer. Edward. Elias. Ethan."

Katherine added, "Edmond. Ebenezer."

Jake joked, "Ebenezer? I'd hate to have that name in school."

A large, familiar black crow soared overhead, cawing loudly. Katherine instinctively looked at the woods and hoped the man would appear. She said, "The man in the woods has a pet crow. That's *his* crow. Now do you believe me?"

Jake looked undecidedly. "How can you tell the difference between one crow from another?"

"Maybe we should have brought Scout and Abra. They would have recognized him." She sat silent for a moment, then said, "Let's drive into Peace Lake and see if there's a store open that sells stationery. I want to write the man in the woods a letter. We can come back later and I'll tape it to the door."

Jake said, "I'm getting really hungry. Want to see if there's a diner open?"

The crow flew back and landed on the hood of the Jeep. Katherine joked, "I think he wants to go, too."

Jake laughed. When he did, the bird flew away into the woods.

*　　　*　　　*

Driving into Peace Lake, they found a restaurant appropriately named Peace Lake Diner. Few cars were parked outside.

Jake pulled into a parking spot in front, and helped Katherine get out of the Jeep. Katherine glanced down the street at the row of antique stores and flea markets. They didn't appear to be open. Jake held the door for her and she walked inside.

A cheery waitress in her sixties came over with menus in hand. "Sit wherever you want."

The walls of the diner were decorated with framed posters of Indiana State High School Basketball Hall of Fame inductees. Jake picked a booth with a print of Rick Mount hanging on the wall. Katherine slid over and made room for Jake, but he sat down across from her.

"Katz, if I sit next to you, it might hurt your ribs turning to look at me every time I say something intellectually stimulating."

Katherine rolled her eyes. "Yeah, right."

Jake read the description at the bottom of the poster and then explained in his own words, "Rick Mount was a high school legend. He was a big-time scorer and had this picture-perfect jump shot."

Gazing around the diner, Katherine observed other posters of famous high school players. "It's like a museum in here for high school legends," she observed. "I hope this diner also has legendary food."

The server came over and read the special—home-cooked chicken and noodles, mashed potatoes and gravy, and a dinner roll.

Katherine's face lit up. "I'm famished. I'll have that, please."

"I'll have the same." The server started to leave and Jake called after her, "Sweet tea for the both of us. Thanks."

"Sure thing," she said.

After they finished their lunch, Katherine leaned over the table and took Jake's hand. "I don't know if you noticed it or not—with all these basketball stars staring at us—but there's a pie menu written on the board."

"Where?" Jake said turning in his seat.

"By the kitchen door."

He squeezed her hand. "Do you see what I see?"

"Yes, coconut cream," Katherine said, and then feigned a British accent, "Would you care for a piece of pie?"

Jake chuckled. "Katz, I don't mean to hurt your feelings, but your impression is terrible. Better stick with your New York accent."

"I beg to differ," she said, pretending to be hurt.

When the server came back with their tab, Jake ordered the pie and coffee.

Katherine asked her, "Wasn't there a basketball legend from Peace Lake?"

The server became very animated. "Yes, his ghost haunts the Lake."

"I've heard about him from my friend Elsa. Sounds like his ghost has helped the town's tourism," Katherine said, amused and referring to the Indiana spirit-hunting website.

The server ignored the comment. "He was really talented, like Rick Mount," she nodded toward the poster. "When I was a teenager, my parents and I went to all his games."

"Rick Mount games? That's really cool," Katherine said.

"No, not Rick Mount. Evan Hamilton. He was Peace Lake's superstar."

Katherine gasped and turned uneasily in her seat.

"Is something wrong, Miss? You look like someone just walked over your grave."

Jake said, "Is there a poster of Evan Hamilton here?"

"Yeah, up front. Behind the cash register."

Jake picked up the tab. "Can we get the coffee and pie to go? Do I pay you or up front?"

The server answered, "I can ring you up front. Be there in a second." She moved away from the table and headed to the kitchen.

Katherine lowered her voice and said excitedly, "E.H. The initials on the knife. Evan's not dead. He's my man in the woods."

Jake and Katherine walked to the register and studied the picture.

Jake asked, "See any resemblance?"

"It's hard to tell. I wish this print was in color."

The server came over and heard the comment. "Oh, there's a color photo right here." She pointed to a glass-covered collage of photos on the check-out counter. "Right there," she pointed.

Katherine inched closer. She studied the picture of a young man with so much promise—a marriage, possible children, and a career.

"Will that be all, folks?" the server asked, putting foam boxes in a bag.

"That's it, thanks," Jake said, handing her several bills. "Your gratuity is included."

The server smiled. "You folks come back now."

Katherine whispered to Jake. "It's him. When I got used to his disfigurement and scars, I remember his brilliant green eye. I'll never forget it in a million years."

"Eye? He only had one eye?"

"Yes, the place where his left eye was supposed to be was closed with scar tissue. This is definitely him."

Jake said, "Let's blow this joint."

They walked out of the restaurant hand-in-hand.

Jake began, "Your fake British accent brought back a memory to me."

"Sherlock Holmes? Sometimes I think you read my mind."

"No, I leave that to your cats," Jake quipped, then quoted: 'There is nothing more deceptive than an obvious fact.'"

"It wasn't too obvious until I found the knife."

"Do you want to go back to the cabin and find a quiet spot near the pond to eat our pie?"

"Sounds like a great idea, but first, we need to find a grocery store. Since Leonard is dead, I wonder if Evan—I finally have a name—has been fending for himself."

"Better be speed-shopping, because in this heat, we'll end up with melted coconut cream pie."

"We can buy ice. I want to pick up groceries for Evan. I also need to buy stationery so I can write him a letter and explain that I'll be delivering weekly supplies.

I'm hoping he'll come out of secret when he sees it's just me."

"Are you going to tell him you know his secret?"

"Yes. And I'm also telling him his secret is safe with me."

"Katz, you really want to do this alone? I'd feel more comfortable if I came with you."

"I'm sorry, Jake, but no. I don't think Evan would hurt me, but just in case I'm wrong, I'll take Miss Glock."

Jake pulled Katherine into an embrace and kissed her. "I love you."

"I love you, too."

# Chapter Nineteen

Katherine parked her new SUV in the graveled driveway of the cabin. She walked around to the passenger door and opened it. Evan Hamilton's high school sweetheart, Marcia Harper Allen, got out.

Marcia asked nervously, "I know I've asked this question a million times, but please tell me again. Evan knows I'm coming?" She held a stack of faded envelopes bound together with a frayed satin ribbon.

Katherine smiled. "Yesterday when I was here, I told him. I also gave him the card you wanted me to deliver."

"How did he react when he saw it?"

"Happy. He was happy. There's a garden bench behind the cabin. It faces the pond. Give me a sec and we'll head that way."

"Where is he?" Marcia asked, looking around.

"He's where he feels most comfortable—in the woods."

"How will he know I'm here?"

"He knows already. I'm sure he's watching us this very moment."

"Ok, but . . ."

"When you see a large crow fly overhead and he lands close by, that's a sign that Evan's near. The crow is Evan's pet."

"I love birds," Marcia said. "When I lived in New Mexico, my late husband and I were avid birders."

Katherine walked to the back of the SUV and lifted the hatch. She grabbed a medium-sized dry-erase board and two markers. She explained, "Evan and I communicate with this."

"Great idea."

Katherine looked in the woods and saw a glimpse of Evan, but knew he was taking his time before making his appearance. "Okay, I'm ready now," she said, closing the hatch. "Let me show you the pond."

The two walked to the front of the cabin—to the newly purchased garden bench—and sat down. The cicadas were singing their song, then quickly fell silent. The early morning fog was lifting and formed a mist over the pond. A mama duck and her ducklings waddled into the water and swam away, quacking.

Marcia said, "It's breathtaking. What an incredible view."

Katherine began, "I rented the cabin until Leonard Townsend's estate closes, then I'm buying the cabin and the surrounding woods, so you're welcome to stay or come out here any time you want."

Marcia's face lit up in surprise. "It's a lovely place, but why aren't you staying here?"

"I've had my share of mother nature," Katherine replied somewhat ruefully. "I want to preserve the woods; there's little over four hundred acres."

"That's a magnificent idea. If I do stay here, I'll insist on paying rent."

"I'm sure we can work something out," Katherine said, then gently switched the subject. "Evan is very sensitive about his scars, but mostly about his missing eye. He's afraid you'll freak out when you see him."

"I'm prepared for a shock," Marcia said seriously, then added, "I think I've already had the shock of my life when you told me a man I thought was dead was very much alive. I'm a trained nurse, so I've pretty much seen everything."

"That's good to know."

"We dated all through high school. We were going to be married," Marcia reminisced. She toyed with the stack of envelopes. A yellow butterfly landed on top of them.

"What are those?" Katherine asked.

"I kept the letters Evan wrote me while he was in Vietnam. Did you know Evan won an athletic scholarship to play college basketball? He also wanted to study to become a doctor."

"What did Evan do in the army?"

"He was a medic."

Katherine's jaw dropped, then she recovered. "That explains why he took such good care of me. I was in so much pain when he pulled me out of my car wreck. He gave me pain meds."

"I can imagine that he was a very good medic. He was very compassionate about the welfare of people and animals. If only Evan would have contacted me when he got back to the states, I would have taken care of him.

Where does he live? He doesn't just sleep in the woods, does he?"

"He said he has a number of cabins he stays in, but he's been using this cabin to take showers. I think he's getting used to it, because he's been sleeping here, as well. I guess I should have told you earlier when I said you could stay here."

"What does he do for food and clothes?"

"Have you ever heard of Tom Hamilton?"

"Yes, I know Tom. He's Evan's cousin."

"Tom owns the Peace Lake grocery store and now delivers food and supplies twice a week."

"That's such an act of kindness, but who pays for it? Over time that would be a lot of money."

"Initially, Evan's uncle, I mean the late Leonard Townsend, financed it."

"I was sorry to hear about Leonard. We called him Lenny. He was ten years older than Evan, and the two of them were thick as thieves."

"I learn something every day." Katherine changed the subject. "I bought Evan new clothes."

"No, you didn't?" Marcia looked amazed.

"I didn't have a clue what size to buy him, but my fiancé, Jake, figured it out. They met last week. Jake also gave him a haircut. We bought him sunglasses and teased him that he looks like Roy Orbison."

"Katz, you have paved your way to heaven."

Katherine became serious. "In Indy there are prosthetic specialists and plastic surgeons that can help Evan, but we'll have to convince him to go for a consultation."

"I think I've got some of the bases covered. First thing I need to do is contact the Veterans Administration. I have to prove that Evan didn't die in Vietnam."

Katherine said carefully, "Marcia, the VA already knows. I don't know how to break this to you, but Evan was honorably discharged after combat service."

"What?" Marcia asked, shocked. "But why did his family tell everyone he was dead?"

"They didn't completely lie. Evan was in a terrible explosion. He was severely injured and in an Army hospital for a long time. He lived in the Philippines for many years and moved back to Peace Lake in 2010. Leonard and Tom made arrangements so that Evan could live here in secret."

"Oh, you wait until I see Tom Hamilton. I'm going to give him a piece of my mind," Marcia said angrily.

"I wouldn't if I were you. Tom would be in quite a pickle if the townspeople knew the haunting of Peace Lake by Evan Hamilton was a big hoax. For now, we need to protect Evan's privacy and keep his whereabouts secret. Okay?"

Marcia nodded. "Yes, of course, Katz. What was I thinking?"

A large crow flew overhead and landed three feet from the bench. He shifted from side-to-side, and hopped up and down. "Caw . . . caw . . . caw."

"Oh, Katz," Marcia said, "Maybe this isn't such a good idea. I've gotten older, and I'm not as trim as when I was a girl. What if—"

Evan walked up behind the bench and put his hand on Marcia's shoulder.

Katherine got up to make room for him. She noticed he was wearing the new khaki shirt and jeans she'd bought him. He'd shaved and had the sunglasses on. His silver hair glistened in the morning sun. Since she had gotten used to him, he looked handsome.

Marcia got up slowly and turned to greet him.

They stood looking at each other, then Marcia collapsed in his arms, sobbing. Evan held her close and was stroking the back of Marcia's hair, comforting her.

Walking to the cabin, a happy tear slid from Katherine's eye. She went inside and poured herself a glass of lemonade. By the time she got to the screened-in porch, Evan and Marcia were sharing the bench, passing the writing board back and forth. Suddenly, Katherine felt a need to see Jake—right away. She just wanted to hold him and tell him how much he meant to her. Then, she'd sign the prenuptial agreement, and they could set the wedding date. Cora, future mother-in-law, could host the reception. Problem solved!

# Chapter Twenty

Katherine was just finishing hand-washing the Haviland china cat dishes when she heard the front doorbell clang. She dried her hands and hurried to answer the door. She'd been expecting Jake and wondered why he'd rung the bell. Usually he disabled the house alarm with his cell and would come right in. She wondered who it could be. Scout and Abra seemed to know. The Siamese zigzagged in front of her, muttering to each other.

"Okay, you two. Explain what's going on—in English, please," Katherine kidded.

Scout cried an emphatic, "Waugh," which seemed to say "hurry up."

Once at the door, Katherine cautioned the cats, "Stay back from the door." Opening it, she was surprised to see Barbie Sanders. Barbie's face was flushed and her eyes were swollen.

"Come in. What's wrong?" Katherine asked.

Barbie walked into the parlor and sat on the settee. Katherine took a chair opposite her.

"It's the kittens." Barbie began to cry.

"What about the kittens?" Katherine asked, suddenly terrified that something horrible had happened to them.

Barbie reached inside her Coach bag and drew out a tissue. Sniffling, she said, "Ever since I took the kittens home, Dewey howls all the time. He won't eat; he won't sleep. I took him to the vet and she said he was depressed."

"Depressed. Why?"

"He misses your cats. I'm sure of it."

Iris trotted in and jumped on Barbie's lap. She reached up with her paw and brushed a tear away. "You're so sweet, Iris." Barbie cried more and Iris got down, not knowing what was wrong with the woman who had rescued her.

Barbie continued, "One of my neighbors—and I don't know which one —called the police. They accused me of abandoning my baby during the day, leaving it unattended while I was away. Can you believe that?"

"Some Siamese can be very vocal, and sound like human infants."

"Ma-waugh," Scout agreed from the next room.

"I hope you explained to the police you have two Siamese."

"I did," Barbie said. "The whole time he was asking me questions, Dewey was yowling at the top of his lungs. The cop said that if I didn't stop the noise, my neighbors could sue me, and my landlord could evict me."

"Barbie, couldn't you give your landlord notice and move to another apartment?"

"Katz, that doesn't solve the problem. I'm sure Dewey would howl wherever I moved."

"I'm so sorry," Katherine consoled, but idly wondered what it would be like to have seven cats.

Jake let himself in and came into the room with a big smile on his face. "Hey, Barbie," then his expression turned to concern. "Has something happened? Why are you crying?"

Katherine explained the landlord situation.

Barbie said in a quiet, sad voice, "I have to re-home my darlings. Katz, I hate to ask you this, because of everything that you've done for me, but would you—"

Jake blurted, "We'll take them. Where are they?"

Katherine's smile broadened in approval. "Yes, Barbie, Dewey and Crowie have a forever home at the pink mansion."

Barbie got up, ran over to Katherine, and gave her a hug.

Katherine said, "Ouch! Not so tight."

"Oh, ha! Ha! I'm sorry," Barbie apologized, then she said to Jake, "They're in my car. We'd better bring them in, because it's so hot outside."

Jake was already at the door, rushing out to Barbie's new red Mustang. Barbie and Katherine quickly followed.

Katherine said to Barbie, "I see you finally got your car back."

"And my bag," Barbie said, nodding at her Coach bag.

Jake opened the door and dragged out the cat carrier. Dewey was shrieking at the top of his lungs. "Mao! Mao!"

"See what I mean?" Barbie said.

"Better say good-bye, Barbie," Jake advised. "These little guys are hot. Gotta get them inside."

Barbie leaned down and said to the kittens, "I love you, my little buddies." Crowie rubbed his face on the grill of the cat carrier; Dewey retreated to the back.

As Barbie walked to her car, Katherine said, "You can come and see them any time. Call me! Text me! I'll send you pics."

"I will," she choked. Barbie eased into the driver's seat and drove away.

Jake carried the cat cage inside and set it down. He sat down cross-legged on the floor. Katherine sat down next to him. Dewey continued to howl.

Scout, Abra and Iris stood nearby. They wore perplexed expressions on their brown masks, which seemed to ask 'why is that cat crying?'" Lilac and Abby appeared out of nowhere to see what was happening.

Jake slowly opened the door and Crowie ran out; he sprang to Katherine's lap and began kneading her arm, purring happily. Lilac and Abby trotted over and took turns licking Crowie's head.

Dewey remained in the back of the carrier. Jake reached in and gently lifted him out. The kitten immediately stopped yowling. Jake flipped him on his back and cradled him in his arms. "What's the problem, little man?" he asked, rubbing Dewey's throat. The kitten reared up and licked Jake on the nose.

Katherine teased. "You missed your calling as a cat whisperer."

Jake smiled, then gave Katherine a serious look. "Looks like we're going to have more in our bridal party?"

"And why's that?" she asked knowingly.

"The bridesmaids outnumber the groomsmen."

Katherine giggled. "I was thinking we could have a small wedding here at the pink mansion with close family and friends—"

"That way the cats can come, too," Jake said happily.

Katherine laughed. "We better not ask Lilac and Abby to be flower girls, because they'll eat the flowers."

"Me-yowl," Lilac protested. "Chirp," Abby seconded.

"Waugh," Scout commanded.

The other cats stopped what they were doing and followed Scout upstairs to the playroom. Dewey and Crowie launched off their new humans' laps and raced behind them.

Katherine leaned into Jake. "You really know how to make a girl happy."

Jake kissed her tenderly on the lips. "Katz, with someone as precious as you, it's been pretty easy."

The End

Dear Reader . . .

Thank you so much for reading my book. I hope you enjoyed reading it as much as I did writing it. If you liked "*The Cats that Watched the Woods*," I would be so thankful if you'd help others enjoy this book, too, by recommending it to your friends, family and book clubs, and/or by writing a positive review on Amazon and/or Goodreads.

I love it when my readers write to me. If you'd like to email me about what you'd like to see in the next book, or just talk about your favorite scenes and characters, email me at: karenannegolden@gmail.com

Amazon author page: http://tinyurl.com/mkmpg4d

My Facebook page is: https://www.facebook.com/karenannegolden

Website: http://www.karenannegolden.webs.com

Thanks again!

Karen Anne Golden

# The Cats that Surfed the Web

Book One in *The Cats that . . .* Cozy Mystery series

If you haven't read the first book, *The Cats that Surfed the Web*, you can download the Kindle version on Amazon: http://amzn.com/B00H2862YG Paperback is also available.

Forty four million dollars. A Victorian mansion. And a young career woman with cats. The prospect sounded like a dream come true; what could possibly go wrong?

How could a friendly town's welcome turn into a case of poisoning, murder, and deceit? When Katherine "Katz" Kendall, a computer professional in New York City, discovers she's the sole heir of a huge inheritance, she can't believe her good fortune. She's okay with the clauses of the will: Move to the small town of Erie, Indiana, check. Live in her great aunt's pink Victorian mansion and take care of an Abyssinian cat, double-check.

With her three Siamese cats and best friend, Colleen, riding shotgun, Katz leaves Manhattan to find a former housekeeper dead in the basement. Ghostly intrusions convince Colleen, a card-carrying "ghost hunter," that the mansion is haunted. Several townspeople are furious because Katherine's benefactor promised them the fortune, then changed her will at the last minute. But who would be greedy enough to get rid of the rightful heir to take the money and run? Four adventurous felines help Katz solve the crimes by serendipitously "searching" the Internet for clues.

# The Cats that Chased the Storm

Book Two in *The Cats that . . .* Cozy Mystery series

The second book, *The Cats that Chased the Storm,* is also available on Kindle and in paperback. Amazon: http://amzn.com/B00IPOPJOU

It's early May in Erie, Indiana, and the weather has turned most foul. We find Katherine "Katz" Kendall, heiress to the Colfax fortune, living in a pink mansion, caring for her three Siamese and Abby the Abyssinian. Severe thunderstorms frighten the cats, but Scout is better than any weather app. A different storm is brewing, however, with a discovery that connects great-uncle William Colfax to the notorious gangster John Dillinger. Why is the Erie Historical Society so eager to get William's personal papers? Is the new man in Katherine's life a fortune hunter? Will Abra mysteriously reappear, and is Abby a magnet for danger?

A fast-paced whodunit, the second book in "The Cats that" series involves four extraordinary felines that help Katz unravel the mysteries in her life.

# The Cats that Told a Fortune

Book Three in *The Cats that . . .* Cozy Mystery series

The third book, *The Cats that Told a Fortune*, is available on Kindle and in paperback. Amazon: http://amzn.com/B00MAAZ3ZU

Autumn in Erie, Indiana means crisp, cool days of adventure. Katherine "Katz" Kendall—heiress to a fortune—settles into her late great aunt's Victorian mansion with her high-spirited feline companions. What better time to host a Halloween party?

Katz sets the stage with spooky decorations, a fortune teller, and even a magician. Scout—a Siamese with extraordinary abilities—fang marks a "Wheel of Fortune" Tarot card. Is it because her person will soon receive millions, or does that card have a more ominous meaning? Although Iris is smitten with the Russian charmer, it's unclear whether he's a lovable rogue, or an opportunistic thief. Katz's new boyfriend Jake and best friend Colleen join in the fun.

Along the way, Katz and her cats uncover important clues to the identity of a serial killer, and Katz finds out about Erie's crime family . . . the hard way.

This fun, fast-paced third book in "The Cats that . . . Cozy Mystery" series involves five extraordinary felines that help Katz solve a crime.

# The Cats that Played the Market

Book Four in *The Cats that . . .* Cozy Mystery series

If you haven't read the fourth book, *The Cats that Played the Market*, you can download the Kindle version or purchase the paperback on Amazon at: http://amzn.com/B00Q71LBYA

Karen Anne Golden's sweet, romantic, cozy mystery "The Cats that Played the Market" is a cat lover's delight. A blizzard blows into Indiana, bringing gifts, gala events, and a ghastly murder to heiress Katherine "Katz" Kendall. With the cats providing clues, it's up to Katherine and her friends to piece together the murderous puzzle . . . before the town goes bust!

It's Katherine's birthday, and she gets more than she bargains for when Colleen and her mum visit the Victorian mansion to celebrate. Handsome boyfriend Jake adds to the joys of the season. After all hell breaks loose at the Erie Museum's opening, Katherine and her five cats unwittingly stumble upon clues that help solve a mystery. But has Scout lost her special abilities? Or will Katz find that another one of her amazing felines is a super-sleuth?

Made in the USA
Lexington, KY
12 April 2015